Crest Contrata

NATHAN GO

FORGIVING
IMELDA MARCOS

Nathan Go was the 2017–2018 David T. K. Wong Fellow at the University of East Anglia. A former PEN America Emerging Voices fellow, he graduated from the Iowa Writers' Workshop and the Helen Zell Writers' Program. His fiction has appeared in *Ploughshares, American Short Fiction, Ninth Letter,* and *The Massachusetts Review. Forgiving Imelda Marcos* is his first novel.

FORGIVING IMELDA MARCOS

FORGIVING IMELDA MARCOS

NATHAN GO

Picador
Farrar, Straus and Giroux
New York

Picador
120 Broadway, New York 10271

Originally published in 2023 by Farrar, Straus and Giroux
First paperback edition, 2024

Library of Congress Control Number: 2023934227
Paperback ISBN: 978-1-250-33575-3

Designed by Patrice Sheridan

Our books may be purchased in bulk for promotional, educational,
or business use. Please contact your local bookseller or the Macmillan
Corporate and Premium Sales Department at 1-800-221-7945, extension 5442,
or by email at MacmillanSpecialMarkets@macmillan.com.

Picador® is a U.S. registered trademark and is used by Macmillan Publishing
Group, LLC, under license from Pan Books Limited.

For book club information, please email marketing@picadorusa.com.

picadorusa.com • Follow us on social media at @picador or @picadorusa

For my father

Author's Note

This is a work of fiction. As is true in many fictional works, aspects of the story were inspired by life. Nevertheless, I want to make very clear to readers that all the characters, and the dialogue, and the locales in this book, and all the events described, are products solely of my imagination.

FORGIVING IMELDA MARCOS

1

LAST NIGHT WHEN I tried again to speak to you, and all I could hear was the silence at the end of your line, your mother took the phone from you and told me that perhaps I needed to give you some more time.

"Because time," I said, "is exactly what I've plenty of."

She wasn't irked at my sarcasm. "I know it must be frustrating," she said. "But considering the circumstances, maybe you should be thankful he doesn't just hang up, that he's still listening. Isn't that what you wanted?"

"I don't know that I wanted anything from him," I said. "I just want to tell him a good story. Something he could maybe use in his career, or that might make his editors proud. Who knows, he could even make a name for himself."

I heard her laugh. She said, "That's not a few wants."

Your mother is a finer person than I am, in almost all respects. Even her English is much better, and I can detect the slightest tinge of the American in her voice, from having lived there with you for so long. She denies it, of course. She'll do everything in her power not to become one of those people who leaves the homeland only to come back years later a foreigner. I can only picture what she looks like now. I've seen movies, you know, seen those wide green lawns of yours with sprinklers that pop up like mushrooms. I imagine your mother carrying copious bags of groceries from the car. She's become bigger. Her hair is as white now as the milk that flows so freely in your land. And even if she tries to dye her hair and to jog around the streets every so often, she can't help herself. You become the landscape you live in, they say.

"Why don't you write to him instead?" she said. "I've always thought of you more as a writer than a speaker."

I told her it would be the same thing, if not worse, since I don't expect you'd write back. And even if you would, given our distance and the way the postal system works in Manila, it would take weeks before I'd get your letter. The anticipation alone would kill me.

"The difference," she said, "is that you'd no longer be waiting. Write everything that you want to say to him. And when he's ready, I'll make sure all the letters reach him somehow."

I told her I'd think about it.

———

You know, you were once very eager to hear your father's stories. I can still remember you as you used to be, with your toes curled up on the footboard, or slumped against me with my lap as your pillow. You were like a little prince, and I, Scheherazade, whose spinning and yarning were aimed at one thing only—to hear you laugh or sigh, so that I could live another day.

"Tell me about the giants!" you'd say, and I'd say, "Not the

Titans again," and you'd say, "Yes, them," because you couldn't quite pronounce their names yet, and I'd pretend to hem and haw, so that you'd beg even louder, and your voice calling out to me would be the sweetest thing I'd ever hear.

But now you and I are much older, and it seems you've fallen back on that thing most natural to men in our family. We become mute toward those we are contemptuous of, especially if the contempt is so intense it starts to rival what was love.

If I may still lend you a piece of fatherly advice, it's to not be too proud to accept help when it is readily offered. Even as I write to you, I'm surrounded by things that sustain me. Things, I'm told, that keep my heart going. I have half a mind to unplug these devices, really, but the better half insists on telling you the story first. Or perhaps this half is really the foolish one, for thinking that someday you'll make good use of it, package it off in some newspaper or shiny magazine with your name on the cover. That someday, when I'm long gone, you might secretly thank me.

But I've gotten way ahead of myself.

What I meant to say, son, is that I'm sure you're perfectly capable of achieving great things by yourself. I've watched you grow, you know, spied you off in the distance, until you transformed into the man so unrecognizable to his own father. And that can only be a good thing! What I'm afraid of—and this is what I really meant to say—is that I might have nothing else to leave you or your mother. Not even memories of our time together. Because, however precious they've become to me these days, I don't presume you'll ever want to recall them. Nor am I asking you to want to recall them. All I ask is that you consider with some openness what I'm about to tell you. And consider my painstaking recollection in these letters not so much a favor on my part. Rather, when the time comes, I hope that your reading them will be an act of kindness for someone who doesn't exactly deserve it.

Where shall I begin?

I guess I'll start my story by addressing what I imagine some of your readers might think. It's particularly important in the beginning to establish a connection, you know, and to set up context. Why, they might ask, should they care about what happened a long time ago in this tiny island nation in the Pacific? And why should they believe in your father—a poor, bumbling, bald high school dropout? Even here, people often think that just because I don't tend to speak my mind, I don't have one at all. And because I've never finished school I can never finish anything worth telling about. I only hope for our sakes that they're wrong.

For a long time, it used to be that one couldn't speak about my country without conjuring up the Second World War: the Battle of Manila, the Bataan Death March, and, of course, General Douglas "I Shall Return" MacArthur. Many forget we were once an American colony—your colony—but you'll never come across this term in history books there, with all their talk of anti-imperialism and being the Land of the Free. Yes, America is a liberator. But often it's also a liberator from the problems it created in the first place. That is the truth, plain and simple.

Now, before you get offended, allow me to just say that, as with any country, America is a type of synecdoche. It is a few individuals who take it upon themselves to stand in for the views of everybody, sometimes accurately, but usually inaccurately. So when I say America, what I really mean to say is your government, at a given time, and its sympathizers. I have to belabor this point because we in the Philippines, in the last decades, have also acquired ourselves a few synecdoches.

I'm talking of course about the late dictator Ferdinand Marcos—or, maybe even more famously, his wife, Imelda: the Lady of the Thousand Shoes. If you've heard only a little about them, don't be dismayed. Even some people here these days don't remember, or choose to remember differently. Perhaps it is a testament to the indomitable will of the human spirit to move on. Dishes have to be washed; clothes to be laundered; babies to be fed and diapered. While tyrants, across the hill and yonder, rise and fall. Or perhaps it is the simple tendency of humans to wax nostalgic, to see only what they want to see of the past. In this regard, I believe, our tiny nation is not much different from yours, or any other. What has happened here could happen there and anywhere else.

To give you one idea of the Marcoses, it might be useful to invoke the memory of a particular British rock band in the sixties. Perhaps you already know this story, but it's from about a decade or so before you were born. While on a tour of the country, the Beatles were requested for an audience with Mrs. Marcos—maybe it was to have lunch with her, or to sing or party at the palace. See, singing was one of Imelda's great passions in life; requesting, however, was not. The Beatles, who failed to show up to the party, soon learned this lesson. Some said it was just a misunderstanding, that they never got the invitation. In any case, the security assigned to them suddenly vanished. Angry mobs, whether deployed by Imelda or simply in awe and fear of her, chased the Beatles down as they tried to depart from the airport.

There is a video out there of the four of them talking about their experience, describing how the airport escalator mysteriously stopped working as they were kicked, booed, and pelted from below. I'm tempted to laugh every time I watch this interview. I tell myself that even a TV show can't invent such insanity. But then I become quiet and turn very, very sullen. Because I realize that the incident also stands in for how I sometimes think and feel about this country.

Forgive me the interruption. I believe we were touching upon the great snubbing of Imelda Marcos, when the nurse, who I didn't hear come inside my room, intruded on my writing. Milo always refers to me as "sir," no matter how many times I remind him not to. I've told him I am neither his boss nor his patron. I don't pay a single centavo to this care home. And last I checked, we haven't started the practice of knighting anyone yet in the Philippines. Not that I would ever qualify.

"Sir," he said, "we have to be careful with our heart."

Careful with *our* heart—that's exactly how he put it! I know he's just trying to be polite, using this quaint third-person-plural construction in Tagalog. But sometimes I'd like very much to think that he speaks to me in metaphors. I'd like to think he's imagining that he and I are somehow fused together. So if I get thirsty or hungry, I could just tug my end of the artery and get his attention right away.

But Milo is straight as a spanner wrench.

Once, I asked if he drank a lot of malted milk while growing up. I was so sure he'd heard this tease many times as a kid. And maybe I regretted asking. Milo didn't get my meaning. "I'm sorry, sir, can you repeat the question?" I wondered if he was feigning ignorance—people who've been bullied, you know, usually acquire a unique set of armor. I told him he happened to share a name with that imported brand of powdered drink—whose commercials, by the way, always feature some athletic kid, when in truth you'd likely get a fat one after feeding him all that malt. Then Milo said to me, "I've actually never had it, sir. I'll have to go try it out for myself. See if it's any good."

He's gone now, my poor conjoined twin. He's left the room. But he's threatened to come back and check on me again if I continue to write rather furiously. So I won't. I promised him, upon our heart, I'd be gentler.

———

Speaking of promises, I told you I haven't forgotten why I'm writing this. I do have a good story to tell you, something I've never told anyone before. It has kept me awake in the past and has especially robbed me of sleep these last couple of days. Between the two of us, I have my own motives for coming out with it only now. But if your editors ask—and if they're good at their jobs, they should—you can always tell them, "Isn't it enough for a father, any father, to want to help his child succeed?"

Now, I don't know how much your mother has told you about the day you left for the United States. I won't be surprised if she hasn't told you much at all, since it was a painful time for both of us, as it would have been for you, too, I imagine, had you been old enough to understand. I don't mean to dwell on this, since it's not the focus of my story. But it is part of a bigger story. And the best way to fit one story among other stories is, I think, always wise to consider.

A long, long time ago, your mother and I worked for a wealthy couple in Manila. I was the family driver and your mother was the nanny. The couple were young and well-liked among their circles. They lived in a bungalow on a street lined with many fig trees. There were five children; the youngest was just a toddler, and taking care of her was your mother's primary responsibility. The wife helped out, too. She mostly stayed at home and she enjoyed gardening during her spare time. The husband, on the other hand, was usually away at work. He was, shall we say, a very important person, and he surely relished it. He had big ideas and even bigger plans.

One thing we learned, on our very first day, was that the husband never liked losing an argument. He might start out all cheery—he did have a healthy sense of humor—but when cornered, instead of agreeing to disagree with you, he'd dig in and throw in everything he had. So once, when he caught me smoking in the yard, I was ready *not* to put up a fight.

"Lito, how can you put that garbage in your mouth?" he said.

"Sir." I immediately threw the cigarette away. "I'm sorry."

"You know it's not good for you," he said.

"I know, sir. It's just that it helps calm me down."

"How?" he said. "That stuff smells awful."

"Yes, sir."

"You know I'm just looking out for you, thinking of your health, right?"

"Okay, sir."

We stood there for a few seconds before I told him that I needed to leave for the day.

"Wait," he said. He looked around and then checked the bedroom window. Seeing nobody there, he lowered his voice. "If you're going to do something wrong, Lito, at least do it right." He reached into his coat pocket and withdrew a pack of Champions, showing me the gold label.

"Thank you, sir," I said, fumbling to pull one out.

From then on, until I quit smoking, I'd always make sure to buy only Champions, even if it hurt my wallet. I preferred that to getting into a situation with him.

Another time, I remember, I'd just picked up his wife from a restaurant when a familiar male voice spoke on the car radio: "If no one is willing to break the silence," the voice said, "then who will? If no one is willing to act, then who will?"

"Ma'am," I said, "isn't that your—"

"I hope he treads lightly," she said.

But as we reached the next intersection, while we stopped for a car that was racing to beat the red light, the husband started a quarrel with the radio host. "The thing you have to know about Imelda Marcos," the husband said, "is that she's a megalomaniac. She's our very own Evita Perón."

"Oh dear," the wife said. "Oh Lord."

He was told to stop. But, as with any independent thinker—and he was fiercely independent—the more he was warned, the more passionate he became.

In those days, it was fairly common for people to suddenly vanish and never be heard from again. We used to joke that if one were homeless, one only had to say something smart about the government to be guaranteed a two-by-two pension room at an undisclosed location. Well, something like that happened to the husband. When martial law was imposed, he was one of the first to disappear. We didn't know where he was, or even if he was still alive. Only a few days later did we get a tip that he was being detained and awaiting trial.

I remember often having to drive his wife and kids and park outside the army barracks where he was being held. Mostly, these visits would happen on a weekday, after the kids were done with school. But it was never up to us. All depended on the whim of the generals in charge and what liquor they'd been drinking the night before. Sometimes, and most inconveniently for you and me, the visits fell on a weekend, when your mother and I normally had our day off and would take you out to the city.

In any case, the husband stayed in jail for a long time. Year after year, his appeals to be released, or even just to stand trial, were turned down. He often refused to eat and the fullness in his cheeks withered away. One day, when he had fallen quite ill, none other than Imelda Marcos herself showed up at his bedside. She stood there with her tall bouffant and took pity on him. "Look what you did to your pretty face," she said. And then, "What do you think about putting our past behind us?"

She agreed to release him as long as he made a promise. From then on, she said, he was to focus only on his health and family. Away and abroad, he was to keep his mouth shut.

Do you still remember that day we drove to the airport in a rickety van? The husband—my boss—rode shotgun while you were in the backseat, guarding all the luggage. His wife followed not far behind in their other car. The children were squeezed in shoulder to shoulder, and your mother made sure they wore their seat belts.

In the van, you wouldn't stop crying. You kept asking questions like, why America? And why wasn't I coming with you? I said, "Because where you're all going, there won't be any need for a driver. Your mother will be the one to take care of my boss in the hospital." Then you asked what you were supposed to do in a country so far away. And I said you would keep your mother company, so she wouldn't be lonely. "Besides," I said, "just think of it as a vacation. You and your mother are coming home as soon as the treatment is done."

Even my boss tried to cajole you, with some orange pastilles. You used to love those, do you remember? They resemble little tongues, soft and granular. I believe they still make them today, though they're not as popular. Anyway, on this occasion you simply wouldn't budge. You kept crying. Then my boss told me he was getting worried. He said you might attract too much attention at checkpoints along the way. Who knew what Imelda would do? She could always change her mind.

So I asked if you believed in Santa Claus, and when you said no, because you'd never seen him or so much as a chimney

before, I asked if you wanted to see him. You gave this some
thought, as if you were pondering a theological question, but after a while you said you weren't interested. So then I asked if you
wanted to see snow, because it was summertime and you were
always complaining about the heat. "Will there really be snow?"
you asked. My boss chimed in and said yes, there would be lots
and lots of snow in Boston. And did you know that each snowflake is different, no two of them alike? You didn't seem to believe
him at first, but he continued in the way only he could, turning
his full attention on you. He began describing the beauty and
intricacy of each pattern of snowflake. And he was still going on
about it when you said yes. Yes! You would like to see snow, okay,
and you would like to visit Boston, and when the time was right,
you'd like to come back home, so you and I could go back to the
mall, where it was always fun and chilly. And then you became
quiet for the rest of that trip, because I guess you were worn out
from crying, and in your mind, the matter had been settled once
and for all.

How I miss that precious way of yours, and how I wish that
things had been a little different. The husband's treatment did go
according to plan. But after his health recovered, he began to visit
different college campuses in the U.S., talking about the dangers
of the dictatorship. He broke the deal with Imelda, saying that a
pact made with the devil was no pact at all.

I suppose he was to be admired on some level, especially for
his steadfastness. But as a father, I couldn't help but worry about
what would happen to you. Long-distance calls were not cheap

back then. So you and I kept communication to a minimum. You were too young to appreciate those calls, anyway, and I didn't blame you. Your voice often panted a quick "Hi" and "Bye" as you hurried off to play with the other kids or perhaps stuff your face with more sumptuous food. Still, my heart soared every time the operator asked if I wanted to accept those charges from overseas. Once, I told her that I'd been waiting, and when I heard her on the line I said I was so happy I could practically kiss her. She must've gotten that a lot.

It was in late May, I remember—because that's also your birth month—and I was visiting my own father up north. He wasn't doing very well then, and because he'd been upset with me, he'd chosen to keep a vow of silence around me—I've already told you about that habit among the men in our family. I prepared him his dinner in the living room and made sure his favorite rattan chair was comfortable. As I did every night, I switched on the TV. That was when my father and I saw the news together.

A man had been shot as he was getting off the plane. He'd been shot right in the head and the all-white shirt he was wearing bloomed crimson from the neck down. His body lay motionless on the ground. My father kept tugging on my sleeves and asking, "Isn't that him?" Of course, at first I was clueless about who he meant. I was more surprised to hear my father talk to me at all. Then I saw the caption on the screen and I felt for my mouth and shook my head. "I didn't even know he was coming home tonight," I said. "Nobody told me anything."

Every Filipino today knows what subsequently took place. The wife, Mrs. Corazon Aquino, came home to Manila with her kids for the funeral. Soon after, she'd decide to take over what her husband had started. Transformed from the soft-spoken woman we all knew, she'd channel her rage and loudly call for protests. Everywhere she went, many shared her grief. The Marcoses would be evicted in a bloodless coup, and Mrs. Aquino would go on to become president.

These events would later be given a fancy name: the People Power Revolution of 1986. But I'd know them as another kind of turning point. I'd remember them as the time I discovered that I would never get to see you again. Because after the dust had settled and the smoke had cleared, I'd eventually learn what your mother had already decided all by herself—that you were to remain in the United States with her, forever.

———

What, you might wonder, has any of this history to do with our story?

Well, when you're approaching the end of the road, life has a very funny way of messing with your head. Time becomes at once very fast and immobile. Memories merge as they collapse; old ones become new ones; new ones become stale. Fear starts feeding up the intravenous tube. You wait out your time or you think of just quitting. And then, once in a while, perhaps stupidly, you think maybe you can still do some good.

Just the other day, Manang Dionisia came by. She's the only one who visits me here. Everybody else is either dead or doesn't want anything to do with your father. Maybe I'm being dramatic. Becoming sappy is another thing that happens when one reaches the end. In any case, Manang Dionisia lives at the ancestral home. She's worked for the Aquinos even longer than I did. She started as their cleaning girl in her teens, and now she's, what?

In her eighties, I think, though still sharp as a tack. She lives in a two-story annex that the Aquinos have built for her and her kids and her grandkids. Loyalty has its perks.

"Leave Milo alone, would you?" she said. "The boy's just being polite. I myself use *we* or *us* when I don't want to sound rude."

"He's also told me I should watch my diet, would you believe? And I said, how could I be a good Filipino and not eat my pork? I'd rather die happy than hungry."

"See? He's looking out for you. He's a good nurse."

"I'm highly suspicious of male nurses."

"And why's that? You think only girls should be nurses?" Manang Dionisia sat upright, as if about to pull out some slogan from under her chair and swat me on the head.

"I was just kidding," I said. "Maybe you're right. Maybe he's just trying to look out for me."

"Correction," she said. "I'm *always* right."

I let her savor this victory lap for a moment. Because I wanted to follow it up with something rather touchy.

"Manang, can I ask you a question?"

"Do I have a choice here?" But she waved at me to go ahead.

"What do you think it is that one must do, you know, to prepare for the next life?"

"Lito," she said, prolonging her vowels. "You're still young. Or at least much younger than I am. And even I don't dwell on those things. Just try your best to get better, okay?"

I had expected something like this, of course, so I pressed a little more firmly. I asked if she thought that most people—sensible people, at least—would use this time to reflect back on their lives and try to settle things.

"I suppose if one's still capable," she said, "then one should."

"But what if, in the process of settling things, you create a new rift with someone, or even several people?"

"Then I suppose you'll have to decide which relationships you prioritize."

"What if you prioritize them all similarly? That is to say, you can't decide on how to prioritize?"

"Then I suppose it's better not to do anything at all, no? But I have a feeling," she said, "there's something else behind this question that you're not telling me."

I studied her expression—in the contrast between those bright black pupils that swiveled ever upward and the lines on her forehead that hung down like roots.

"Do you ever find yourself," I asked, "thinking back to the time Madam got sick with cancer, before she passed away?"

"Not particularly."

"Would you ever remember a certain day when Mrs. Aquino did something that those closest to her thought she shouldn't have done?"

Manang Dionisia said nothing this time.

"If you can just help me out here. I can't seem to tell anymore if it was just a dream I've made up, or if I'm conflating several memories."

She looked away, resting her gaze on a pot of plastic daisies.

I continued. "It's just, I've been thinking. What had taken place might serve a greater purpose if it's no longer kept a secret. I think the knowledge can be of good use to some people. A lot of people, actually. Lessons could still be learned."

"You've sworn," she said, "to the same family that has taken care of you for so long, that has given you not just a livelihood but a good life, that you weren't going to talk about it, ever. But you already know this, Lito. So I'm not sure what it is you really want from me. Is it confirmation that the event actually happened? Or are you looking for something else? Some permission, perhaps, some reassurance that a coward may go ahead and do cowardly things?"

She sat there, picking lint off her frayed flannel pants. At one point, she hummed a low tune before she caught herself and stopped. Then she said, "It's getting late."

I have been called a coward many times before in my life. Mostly during my adolescence—I was a late bloomer in school, if not everywhere else, and consequently I've never been gifted with any kind of foresight. A few of those times, though, were in my adulthood, with your mother's use of the term being a particular kiss of death—but I fully admit I deserved that one. And now, in my twilight years, a gift from my only remaining friend to add to the collection.

It's just as well, isn't it? Then I truly have nothing else to lose by telling you the story. As improbable as the events might sound to anybody, to the people in this country especially, at least I know they did occur. Perhaps it might help for the story to be shared by someone of your credentials—a journalist from an esteemed American newspaper. Or possibly, given how things are nowadays, it might just hurt. But here I am again, getting way ahead of myself. I'll leave it for you to decide, by the end of the story, what you want to do with it. And I'll leave to fate whatever it wants to do with me.

2

IT HAPPENED OVER a holiday weekend.

That much I remember, because I wasn't supposed to be working that day. But Mrs. Aquino called me on my cell phone on a Friday night and asked if I wanted to do a shift. Now, a *shift* was an old term carried over from the time Mrs. Aquino was still president. Years earlier, she had needed to be driven back and forth from the Arlegui Mansion to the Malacañang Palace, where she held office. Then from the palace she'd go to convention halls, hotels, homes of dignitaries. Or to the hangar, where a helicopter waited in the event of severe traffic or if she needed to leave Metro Manila. One driver could not have met all those needs. So there were several of us, working in shifts.

After her retirement, however, she chose to retain only me as her personal driver. Though it's true I had worked for her the longest, it is with a certain pride—as well as pure conjecture on my part—that I say she retained me because I was the most dependable and, I'd like to think, the most companionable. In any case, the years following her retirement from public life were not easy for a driver. There were fewer and fewer errands to run. Mrs.

Aquino could only attend so many fundraisers or meet with so many friends at places properly equipped with security. Even her children had all grown up and left the house. Some had given her quite the precocious grandkids. But again, there were only so many times she could visit them.

On that particular Friday night when she called, I was alone at my apartment watching a movie, or maybe catching up on some reading. I had, in fact, taken the whole week off to "see friends and relatives." In reality, I just didn't want to show up for work, day after day, scrounging for things to do. So you could imagine I was rather elated when I heard that she needed me for the weekend. She didn't specify the reason and it would've been presumptuous of me to ask. But I assumed it had something to do with tinkering around the house. See, I had become quite the handyman, if I may say so. I'd forced myself to learn a few tricks in basic plumbing and electric wiring, and had even begun to share with her a genuine interest in her garden. Still, I had the feeling that every time she asked for my help, she was merely looking out for me. Whenever I could, I tried to reciprocate with the dignity she'd afforded me.

"Yes, ma'am," I said in a controlled voice. "I think I could manage to swing by this weekend."

By seven o'clock the next morning, I was at her bungalow at Times Street. I'd parked my motorcycle and had entered the gate quietly using the set of keys entrusted to me. I was in the sunroom, spraying a mist of water on her beloved cattleyas, when I heard my name. I turned around and at first thought I was staring at her nurse, for she was wearing a flowy white dress. But it was Mrs. Aquino herself, looking as if she had sleepwalked her way in. She asked if I was ready. And when I replied, "Ready for what?" she said, "To leave."

"How are you feeling today, ma'am?" This was a most mundane question, one that ordinarily I would've avoided. But what I'd really meant to say was "Are you fully cognizant today?"—which might seem patronizing or unkind on my part, but was really the opposite. I just wanted to make sure that she truly wished to leave the house at such a godforsaken hour.

Clearly, she didn't take it that way.

"Not you, too," she said, and sighed.

But she soon apologized, saying she was just getting a bit tired of that question. It was as if everybody around her had suddenly turned into a doctor, prying about her symptoms, or giving her their own dubious remedies and cures. Or yet, she said, they'd turned into basketball coaches, telling her that she needed to keep up the brave fight. It was why she was never going to another party or family gathering for as long as she lived. Such occasions were never conducive to anything but professing how well one was doing. "But of course," she said, "you won't have known all these silly thoughts I've been putting up with lately."

"I understand, ma'am." I placed the spray bottle on the table as gently as I could. "I'm afraid there's only one other thing," I said. "I happen to have just started changing the car's oil."

"Haven't you just done that recently?"

"They recommend every three months," I said. But upon remembering that I'd changed it barely a month ago, I added, "Or thereabouts, ma'am. Depending on usage."

This probably sounded a little fishy, too, as the car had barely been used. And these days, with synthetic oils and engines being what they are, the SUV really could have gone on longer without such nitpicky maintenance. But Mrs. Aquino sensed my unease and once more tried to spare me.

"Okay," she said. "How long should we expect to wait?"

I checked the clock on my cell phone. "About forty minutes, ma'am, to an hour."

She was pacing the stretch of the sunroom now. She stopped every so often to adjust her glasses, which I'd heard were made of titanium, but lately I thought they looked heavy on her nose. I almost wanted to lift their burden off her and tell her she should go back to sleep. It really was far too early.

"Let's take the Crown, then," she said.

"Ma'am?"

"Don't tell me you've also just changed the oil for that one!"

"No," I said. "In fact, I don't remember the last time it had a tune-up."

"Well, it seems we don't have a choice here."

"May I ask, ma'am, where we're going?"

"To the house of an old acquaintance." She took out from her purse a baronial envelope from which she read, "Poblete Street. Baguio City."

"Baguio, ma'am?" It was at least a six-hour drive away.

"That's why we need to leave now. So we can make it back by nighttime." She crossed her arms.

"Right, ma'am. I'll fetch you your nurse."

"Don't bother," she said. "I gave her the day off."

By then all sorts of red flags had sprung up, but my mind was too constricted to think of another way to stall. Besides, who was I to defy her? I thought the best thing to do was to let her children know, so they could deal with their mother in that stern but pardonable way permitted of a member of the family.

Just a couple months before, in fact, I was given a directive to that effect. It had made me quite uncomfortable, actually. Mrs. Aquino had slipped and fallen while climbing a set of stairs during a house party. She was not seriously hurt, thankfully. But over the course of that evening I was called aside by her daughter Kris. From that day forward, she told me, I needed to report any "incident" or "unusual behavior" on Mrs. Aquino's part, as Mrs. Aquino apparently had been skipping her pills at times. In short, I was made into a double agent, working for both mother and daughter. "But you understand why we must do this," Kris had said. "We're just looking out for her."

This was what I was trying to juggle that morning, so that only when I got seated inside the Crown did I realize that something was missing: my cell phone. I had left it in the sunroom. I really was not cut out to be a spy.

"What is it now?" Mrs. Aquino asked from the backseat.

I told her what I'd forgotten, not seeing any reason to lie. I said I was just going to take a moment.

"Don't bother," she said. "Just use mine if you need to."

"But ma'am, if someone were to call me?"

"Like who?" she said, rather impatiently.

When I didn't respond right away, she said, "I know what you're thinking."

"Ma'am?"

"Lito, let me ask you. How long have you worked for me?"

"Since I was in high school, ma'am."

"Since I *put* you through high school. Before you quit."

"That's right, ma'am."

"And what has Kris ever done for you?"

A moment passed before I turned on the ignition. The engine sputtered. Then the Crown crawled out of the garage.

———

I'd like to pause here for a second. I want to say something about my high school days and to somewhat defend my independence, a matter of no small pride to me. Because even though Mrs. Aquino did support me in my failed pursuit of a diploma, the support was partial and mostly indirect.

First, I was a working student back then, but she always accommodated my schedule. She herself would drive the children around whenever I had to take off for my classes and exams. Second, the wages she paid me were higher than the going rate. So in effect, combined with my thriftiness, I received a surplus that I turned into an allowance for books and meals and such things. Third, in the event that I still didn't have enough funds to cover all my tuition, which happened only once or twice, an anonymous donor would swoop in to settle the balance. I never found out the donor's identity. But then, who else could it be?

So even though I said that Mrs. Aquino's support was "indirect" and at best "partial," please understand that I was also by no means being ungrateful. Mrs. Aquino, after all, like any practical and sensible woman of her generation, didn't just throw money around. I suspect that when she said she had put me through high school, well, at the time, accuracy wasn't exactly at the forefront of her mind.

———

Nor is it actually on the top of my mind now, if I may be perfectly honest, while we're on the topic.

Since moving into this care home, I've been giving some thought to how I should properly tell you the story, as it all happened quite a few years ago. I was having coffee one afternoon, my usual kapé barako, when I came across an article in the newspaper. I won't tell you which local newspaper; it's beside the point. But the article struck me as a bit false. It read as a bit too effusive, as if written by a junior officer or agent trying to get a promotion in government.

The words he'd chosen were more positive than neutral. He'd say something like "the successful inauguration," instead of "the inauguration" or just stating the time and place. The quotes he included came from just one person, who also happened to have deemed the inauguration a success. In short, it made me question the author's true intentions.

Which then made me wonder—in telling you the story, what happens if I forget a few details here and there? What if I embellish a few things, you know, to make it more exciting or interesting, as any good storyteller would do? What if I shuffle some events, or even invent them, but the overall intention is still to make you understand a truth that couldn't be arrived at any other way?

The one thing I realized that afternoon, aside from the fact that kapé barako doesn't taste bad when served cold, was that we all need to be more skeptical. It's hard enough to know someone's true intentions, let alone judge whether those intentions are pure or tainted. We should never trust someone who insists he's telling you the whole truth. And we should always take his stated intentions with a grain of salt. The real intentions, more often than not, are the ones lurking underneath the surface.

———

Here's a little digression into your lineage.

My father, your grandfather, when he was still alive, was a highly skeptical person. This is another trait that runs deep among the men of our family.

My father did not believe in the Church. He did not believe in government. And he most certainly did not believe in me. You can only imagine the sheer frustration, and even terror, of a child who comes running home one day with a blackened eye, only to be blamed and punished for having "started the fight."

See, I was—as I am now—quite pudgy. But I am a pudgy fellow of the peaceful kind. Perhaps rather like elephants, who, as big as they are, would prefer to leave alone a tiny mouse who has found his way into their food rather than stomp on him. That's not to say that I'd prefer to abandon my food. Indeed, food always sustained me. It used to be the friendliest and warmest thing I'd ever find at our house.

And what about your grandmother? Well, my mother died when I was just two years old, so I never had any memories of her, nor did I have any siblings who might have shared such memories with me. Her tragic death, which I'll get into in just a minute, had a profound influence on my father, and consequently on me. As harsh an environment as the one my father had created at home, it was the only thing I knew as a child. Being motherless, I thought, was the normalest thing in the world.

To illustrate, I never was a kid who wondered about procreation. But when I was once cornered by an older classmate and asked to explain the mystery of where I'd come from, I said the process was something like that of a Xerox machine. You just need one person to churn out another. Adults around me, after all, were always telling me how I was a striking copy of my father.

As for him, his wife's death would eventually turn him into a believer. Not exactly a less skeptical man but a different kind of skeptic altogether. What I mean to say is this.

He had inherited from his own father a sugar mill in Moncada, a town not far from where we used to live. Persnickety as he was, he was actually very good at his business. He always knew just how much sugarcane to buy in anticipation of the next season's demand.

However, there were two things that had always cut into his profit: the bribe for the tax collector, and the "donation" for certain Communists active in the area. If he didn't pay either one of them, all kinds of trickery could be done to him. His business permit could be "misfiled" by the authorities, or they could cite obscure provisions in the law that could then be used to pad his tax bill. On the other hand, if he didn't give in to the Communists' demands, he could find the tires of his truck mysteriously punctured, or the water pipes connecting to his mill suddenly severed.

Of course, he loathed both sets of people. And that loathing would only turn into anguish when, one day, an army brigade accidentally met a band of insurgents in our town. The insurgents resisted showing their IDs and one thing led to another. That morning, my mother was buying fruit at the market. She and five other civilians were caught in the crossfire.

The randomness of her death was what most pained my father. His mind simply could not wrap around the idea that she had died for no good reason. As I said, he was a skeptic. So he himself began investigating the "truth" of what had happened.

He cut out newspaper articles that mentioned anything related to the army brigade or the local Communist movement. He became so obsessed with tracking down the latter that eventually he found one of their camps, tucked away in the mountains of Zambales. The leader of that group turned out to be a retired priest—not any ordinary priest, mind you, but a priest said to be endowed with magical powers. My father would one day set out to meet him, with a picture of my mother in one pocket and, in the other, a butterfly knife.

———

Back to our earlier story: I remember the road along Epifanio de los Santos Avenue being devoid of traffic, as it was a holiday. Mrs. Aquino and I were making good time toward Balintawak, often seen as the older northern boundary of Manila.

When I made a turn to enter the intersection, we heard a squeal from the front wheels and Mrs. Aquino asked if we should be concerned. I told her the car was probably low on steering fluid but that we should be okay. "We just have to rely on good old pawis steering," I said, which means "sweat" in Tagalog. That made her laugh.

It is a delicate matter, though, sometimes, to joke around with your employer, especially when she is, or used to be, the president of a republic. In this regard, I was lucky to have known her before she assumed office. Still, there were times when I made a miscalculation, like on the way to a joint session of Congress where she was to address the nation on live TV. I told her a joke, something to do with the difference between Congress and the Manila Zoo. But Mrs. Aquino was nervously practicing her speech, and I should've known she wasn't likely to appreciate some wisecrack at the expense of those men—and a few women back then—who were to be her main audience inside the hall. Consequently my joke was met with silence and, I believe, with a hint of disappointment.

I wonder if you'd be able to appreciate my humor, by the way, since I think Filipino humor is quite unique. It tends to be self-deprecating, and plays on words in ways other people wouldn't consider clever. On balance, however, I find that regardless of culture, most people forgive you for attempting to make them laugh. If you don't take yourself too seriously, others feel encouraged not to worry about being judged. Humor, I guess, is a kind of laxative—prying loose the most constipated of people.

"Lito," Mrs. Aquino said when we were driving along North EDSA. "What was that monstrosity we just passed by? It looked something like a flying saucer. I don't believe I've ever seen it before."

"Sky Dome, ma'am. It just opened last month."

"Do you know what's inside?"

"Oh, it's just the newest addition to the mall. Some shops and arcade games, I'd imagine. I believe they're trying to appeal to the teenagers, ma'am, get them into the malling habit. But I've yet to go myself." I smiled. "I'm afraid I'm a little past the age of their target audience."

"Ah, I see."

"Is everything okay, ma'am?"

"Yes," she said. "Everything's fine." She sounded a little hesitant.

And that's the other thing I've learned about humor in my job. Judging how another person reacts to a joke can serve as a gentle gauge of her mood. What I sensed, driving Mrs. Aquino out of Manila that day, was that she preferred to keep to herself, for whatever reason.

So I quickly decided to let her be. After all, I thought, we tend to become more introspective as we age.

———

I can assure you, however, that over the years Mrs. Aquino and I have had many, many wonderful conversations, which I shall always cherish. In terms of company, I really couldn't have asked for a better passenger. I remember one day, after she had just come back from the Vatican, when she told me that the Pope had taken her aside and whispered in her ear: "There are some people, Cory, that God has given special gifts. And you are one of them."

She said that she had blushed, because she couldn't imagine herself to be someone gifted with anything. "But then," she said, "aren't popes supposed to be infallible?" If only, she lamented, she'd had the courage to ask what gift it was she allegedly possessed.

"Perhaps modesty, ma'am," I said. I thought she was plenty courageous in her own right.

"Or perhaps beauty," she joked.

But my personal favorite was the conversation—or series of conversations—we had about the city of Manila. I might have mentioned to you already that I grew up near Moncada, which is a town about one hundred fifty kilometers up north. Many

Manileños have a term for someone like me: *provinciano*. Don't worry, because the dislike was mutual. I simply could not understand how people could live in such clogged streets, with crime, smog, and snobbery to add to the ambience.

Indeed, in my first few years driving in Manila, I'd always get lost and have to park by the curb. That was when I'd encounter some of these snoots who thought themselves too important to help with directions. They'd treat me like an idiot for not grasping the manifest logic of streets that abruptly end in a concrete wall, where drivers have to pass through an alley to go around the wall, with no warning that the alley itself is actually one-way, and when, finally, the right detour is found, a train junction appears out of nowhere.

"It's as if the whole city was designed by a spiteful kid trying to draw up a maze," I told Mrs. Aquino once, when I had to stop and consult a map.

But she merely nodded and said that she agreed, even though I believe she would've more or less considered herself a Manileño. "Do you want to hear a story about the city?" she asked. "It's rather a bleak one, I warn you."

"I'm used to bleakness, ma'am," I said. "Please go ahead."

Manila, she went on, was once called the Pearl of the Orient. It was known, among other things, for its beautiful architecture, modern buildings, efficient streetcars, and historic Spanish churches made of lava rock. But during the Second World War, the city became a target for the Americans. Everyone knew the Japanese weren't going to give up Manila without a fight, she said. But fewer people knew, even today, that Manila could actually have been spared. She explained that the Americans could've gone straight to Okinawa to soften the Japanese defenses. It was just that General MacArthur insisted that it was his personal responsibility to liberate the Filipinos, and hence, Manila.

The result, Mrs. Aquino said, was that both Japanese and American forces reduced the city to rubble. The Americans dropped many, many bombs. And the Japanese soldiers, defiant to the end, massacred anyone who came their way. More than a hundred thousand civilians died in the process, and almost all the buildings were destroyed. Only Warsaw suffered a worse fate during that period.

"We also have ourselves to blame for Manila's current condition," she said. "But you have to understand, we didn't exactly inherit the Garden of Eden."

It was my moment of epiphany, for I'd never before viewed Manila as an underdog. From then on, I'd cut it a little more slack whenever I had to make an unexpected detour. I'd be more understanding when I couldn't take the car out because the license plate ended in the wrong number that day. Every year, I grew to like Manila more and more. And now I've even come to miss it.

———

Last night, partly because I kept reminiscing to you about my past, I dreamed about a geology lesson in my fourth-grade science class. On the blackboard, in big, bold letters, were the words *Igneous. Metamorphic. Sedimentary.*

When I woke up this morning, I quickly jotted down the dream so I'd remember to tell you about it. I know I'm being a tad childish here, or perhaps it shows you just how much goes on in my life nowadays. But I hope you'll appreciate this, as someone who plies words for a living. It's not so much the scientific aspect of those rocks that got me excited—although I did like science, as long as no numbers were involved. It's the language aspect. Even at that age, which I guess would've been around ten or eleven, I particularly delighted in the lesson. I did not quite understand why at the time. Only, I recall having a reaction to those three words that was so visceral that—and I know this is going to sound ridiculous—it could be summed up as *delicious*.

I figured the order had as much to do with this pleasure as the sound of each individual word. *Igneous*, being the first, is also the most defiant, won't you agree? It calls to mind such relatives as *ignoble*, *ignite*, and, of course, *ignorant*. The stress on the initial syllable announces itself. And it's perhaps no surprise that this is the hottest of all rocks, having just emerged from the volcano. *Metamorphic* introduces itself more gently, mellowly, matter-of-factly. Its stress has moved to the second-to-last syllable. Like the geological formation, it has gained some weight: it now has one more syllable than *igneous*. But finally, *sedimentary* is the fattest of them all, the longest word to pronounce. Its stress—though still on the third syllable—can be seen as having moved even farther than in *metamorphic*. And this makes total sense, doesn't it? Sedimentary rocks have had thousands of years to cool off. Its heat, so to speak, has also moved farther inward.

I told Milo the same thing when he came to see me, and to my surprise the boy did appreciate my explanation. When I asked if he'd had similar experiences as a kid, he took only a moment before coming up with an answer. "Hagdang-hagdang palayan," he said. "I know it's in Tagalog, so bear with me here as I pronounce it slower, accentuating the stresses. It should sound something like *hug-dúng hug-dúng pal-luy-yán*. I wonder if you can hear the percussive beat in the repetition of those first two words. There's almost a release when we get to the softer *l* and *y* sounds of *palayan*. Would you be surprised if I told you that the term refers to 'rice terraces' and *hagdang-hagdang* simply means 'steps'? You can really hear the clip-clop of someone's feet ascending or descending those terraces."

"Isn't language just wonderful?" I asked Milo.

"I wouldn't know, sir," he replied. "I was never good at it. Never understood my poems."

"I bet you understand more than you think you do. A lot of it is instinctual, unconscious. It involves your ear as much as your mind."

"I believe you, sir. I just don't understand it. But I liked the way you broke things down."

"What does your name mean, again?" I asked, trying to be more sensitive this time.

"Sir?"

"Milo. What does it mean, I'm curious to know."

"Oh, I looked this up once, sir. But there's no clear explanation. It could be from German, meaning 'mild' or 'calm.' Or it could also mean 'merciful,' from another language, I forgot which. Anyway, my parents never told me what or who they named me after."

"It's a beautiful name," I said. "Just listen to it: *Milo*. There really is a calmness and mildness about it. You'd have been a very different person if you were called something else. I don't think I'd have liked you as much."

"Oh, thank you, sir," he said, taking a bit to recover. Then, looking as if he'd just realized something, he asked, "What about you, sir? What does your name mean?"

———————

Well, Angelito is probably obvious, though not necessarily self-evident in me. My surname, Macaraeg—that's the remarkable one. It comes from the root word *daig*, which means "beat." But the question is, does it mean "to beat" or "to be beaten"?

I admit that most names indeed have positive connotations. So in my case it probably means "to be victorious," especially given its Tagalog prefix. But wouldn't it be refreshing, if not downright more useful, for someone to bear a lasting mark, a kind of generational reminder, that something so tragic once happened, something so sorrowful, that a whole clan needed to learn from it and rise above their past?

In any case, I think names usually play a bigger role in shaping who we become. Isn't it funny that the two people I keep bringing up here—Mrs. Aquino and Mrs. Marcos—both have names that reflect their personalities, if not their whole lives? Mrs. Aquino was Maria Corazon, which means something like "the heart of Mary." And Mrs. Marcos, of course, is Imelda, which, I discovered after some prying, means "powerful fighter."

And then we have you, José Antonio.

I don't know which surname you've chosen to keep for yourself. Sometimes I even wonder if you've retained the classic Spanish name, or perhaps you've changed it to something like John Anthony. Life would probably be much easier there with a name like that.

But did you also know that you were named after your grandfather—my father? I wonder if your mother has ever told you. He's dead now, bless his soul. But I realized I kept going on and on about his life the other day, for no particular reason. I'm sorry about that. Once I finished writing, I couldn't understand why I'd brought him up in the first place. Now I seem to know and remember.

Son, there's something I've been meaning to ask you, something I've never asked anyone before. I admit that this time you'll be doing me a favor, as I may never have the chance to tell you about it ever again. If you allow me, this thing will make sense only if I first share with you another story. It is not a very long story, thankfully, though it is rather a complicated one, and for that I apologize. But I promise you, in the end, everything will come together.

3

IT ALL STARTED with an egg.

At least, that was what my father told me, a few days after he met Ka Noel in the mountains of Zambales. *Ka* is short for *kasama*, or "comrade," and it is what Ka Noel preferred to be called rather than the name he once used as a priest.

"Here," he said to my father, handing him the brown egg. "Hold it tight."

My father hesitated. He had just stumbled upon the rows of nipa huts in the jungle that evening and didn't yet know what to make of the guerrillas. And, of course, he didn't want to make a mess of an egg.

"You have a lot of fear in you," Ka Noel said. "And hatred." My father gritted his teeth and clenched his fists. "Harder," Ka Noel said. "Give it all you got."

The man is an old fool, my father thought. And yet there he was, surrounded by hundreds, if not thousands, of Ka Noel's followers. They all carried guns. My father had traveled with nothing but a knapsack of food supplies, which had run out by the time he found the village. So he'd thrown it into a ravine and had come as himself, with only a watch and his round spectacles to his name. Perhaps the villagers thought *he* was the crazy one.

"You can let go now, brother."

"What?"

"This," Ka Noel said.

My father looked down and realized that his fists were turning blue. Inside one of them was the egg, unbroken.

"When I heard what happened, I was very sad," Ka Noel said. "My men go down to Moncada once in a while to sell our crops. We know we're being watched, but we don't have a choice. If I'd known, however, that . . ." He breathed in deeply. "I'd have insisted we all go hungry instead. Brother, trust me. We would never hurt ordinary people, because they're just like us. We *are* the people."

At this, my father's wrath only intensified. Before he could restrain himself, the egg in his hand flew out and up toward Ka Noel's face. But it bounced right back and landed on my father's feet. It was still whole, my father swore to me, and because they were sitting outside the camp, the egg not only took on the glow of the fire, but also seemed to glow from within.

My father was about to pick up the egg when a familiar knife flashed in front of his eyes. It was the butterfly knife he had hidden and strapped near his shoes. In a moment he thought he was going to die. And that was all very well, for it was what he had expected, showing up by himself this way. It was secretly what he had wished for. He prepared to close his eyes when the blade was turned around to face him hilt-first.

"You have come to seek justice," Ka Noel said. "And there is no better justice than to meet the man responsible for the death of your wife. You have come to kill me, brother, this I know. So kill me."

———————

In almost every religion or organized belief system, there is a tradition of telling one's conversion story. Usually it involves extreme opposites: from profligate prince to enlightened ascetic; from drug addict to doting parent; from criminal to saint; from Paul to Saul. Embellishments and exaggerations not only abound but are to be expected. Though the listener can take the story with a grain of salt, even spoonfuls of it, that doesn't matter. What matters, and what cannot be contested, is that, in the mind and heart of the convert, the spiritual experience did occur. The encounter is genuine and supremely felt. Therefore, when he or she tells you the story, the convert is not just doing it as a favor, extending you the invitation, so to speak, to experience your own. Rather, every time the story is retold, the convert relives his ecstasy.

I had just entered high school when my father told me his story. Of course, back then I didn't view it so abstractly. Instead, I was rather amused, at first, that a grown man could narrate such a wacky tale. I thought it possible that he was kidding or teasing me. But I soon realized that he was very serious. Then I thought maybe he had just gone off the deep end. This amused me, too, because by that time, I didn't care much about him anymore. In my dreams, I had fantasized that my father was already dead.

You have to understand the mentality of not only a teenager here, but a teenager who has been abandoned again and again. So consumed was my father by his search for my mother's killers that, when I was growing up, it was not uncommon for him to disappear without telling me or anyone else. For days, I'd have to fend for myself. There would be food inside the fridge, mostly soup and viands from the carinderia, along with store-bought bread. There'd be some money left on top of our piano, and in the beginning, a note stapled to the bills—I've forgotten the exact wording, but there was always some excuse about leaving on urgent business and not wanting to wake me up, and so forth. But after a while he stopped leaving even those notes. I had a feeling that even he was embarrassed about lying so often to a child.

Though my father's disappearances had become quite common, I still knew, somehow, that they were not normal. Perhaps I realized it when my teacher sent us home with our report cards, and, rather than tell the truth of my situation, I forged my father's signature. I got caught because my penmanship was too poor to pass for an adult's. My father was called in. I was so sure that I'd be reprimanded and suspended.

Instead, he made a scene about being insulted for *his* bad penmanship, and how dare my teacher accuse his son—me—of being anything but an upright student. That secret wink, no matter how perverse, was one of the few moments of bonding that I recall between us.

I admit that sometimes being left alone at home, with a stash of corn chips and chicharrones by my side, and the promise of endless hours of TV and no homework, did not bother me so much. In fact, it's possible that I even looked forward to my father leaving on these occasions. When days had passed since his last trip, and I'd get the sense that he was making preparations anew, I'd start to behave my best. I'd make a big show of doing all my assignments while he could still serve as witness, as if to tell him, "See, nothing to worry about, I'm a big boy." And then when that glorious morning came, unannounced, the bills on top of the piano, the fridge filled with food, I'd accept it all as my "reward." I wouldn't invite any friends over—not a single soul—not so much out of concern for protecting my father's secret, but because I was greedy. Maybe this is how introverts are born.

In any case, one day I had been watching Tom chase Jerry over and over when I heard a knock outside. I knew it couldn't be my father, because he had keys. If it had been him, I'd have heard the clatter of the gate being opened and his car sliding into the driveway. Besides, he rarely came back when the sun was still up, as if he were trying to make the most of his trip. I ignored the knocking at first. Then it became relentless enough that I couldn't continue watching TV. So I put on my slippers.

This woman, standing by the iron rails, I knew to be my aunt.

Strange sentence, perhaps, but it expresses precisely our relationship up to that point. She had on large sunglasses, her hair was neatly combed though not styled, and she always spoke softly, as if she were preserving her voice for choir. I'd met her only once or twice before in my life. I believe now that she was indeed my father's sister—many years later, she'd appear again at his funeral. Back then, she could have been anybody that my father wanted me to call "aunt." Anyway, this aunt said rather grumpily that she'd been knocking for a long time. She asked me to let her in. As soon as I complied, she took it as permission to barrage me with a million questions.

"Where's your father?"

"Out on business."

"Where to?"

"Not sure."

"Anyone else here?"

"Nope, just me."

"This happen a lot?"

"Sometimes."

"How long is he gone for?"

"Don't know."

"Are you okay?"

"Yeah."

"You sure?"

Somehow, this last question, though merely iterative, had a different force, perhaps ending in a higher pitch, perhaps accompanied by a raised eyebrow, because it knocked me silly. I started to cry.

"Does he ever hurt you?"

"Whaa-t?"

"Does he punch or kick or slap you?"

I shook my head.

"Does he shout at you? Call you names?"

I shook my head.

"Does he ever smell?"

"Whaa-t?"

"Like he's been drinking. Lord, I don't know how to describe. Something yeasty. Stale. Maybe smells like pee?"

"You mean alcohol," I said.

She laughed and wiped her eyes. And then this aunt who always spoke so softly suddenly wrapped her arms around me. It felt weird at the time, you know, like she was trying both to suffocate and comfort me. I was eight years old, I remember. And I had just received my first hug.

Not long after she left and my father returned, he agreed to put me up in a boarding school for boys located in the next town. I think he was talked—or rather, threatened—into it by my aunt, because she also gave me her phone number, and said that I should call her if ever I found myself in trouble. In any case, my father and I never had a serious conversation about my transfer, as if it had always been part of his grander plan.

Now, when I say "boarding school," I don't mean to evoke the version that you might have there in the States. You know, wealthy parents sending their kids to private schools that offer posh accommodations. Ours might actually have been a case of mistranslation, or even misguided ambition, because "boarding for a school" is perhaps closer to the meaning. My boarding school was a cheap dormitory not connected with the nearby school whose students it supposedly served.

In fact, I think most school boards would be appalled if they knew the conditions at our boarding school. The two-story house was tucked at the end of a blind alley and its foundations were slowly being squeezed out by the roots of a monstrous talisay tree. To save on bills, electricity was switched off after nine o'clock every night and the galley kitchen locked up. Of course, this did not deter the boys from finding their own fun. Each room shared a long, dusty balcony, from which we could leer at the passersby below. On evenings when the rain had cleared and the moon had come out, our neighbor's water buffalo would show up for a bath. No sooner would he have dipped into his pothole than his hot flank would be pelted by paper arrows from the slingshots of the little devils above.

Still, a few good things came as a result of living at the boarding school. For one, I always found company in the form of my roommate, who, although he spent most of his time sleeping and never once cleaned his part of the room, calmed me down with the mere sound of his snoring. Then there was the utter lack of TV, which was painful in the beginning, but eventually forced me to seek out other kinds of entertainment. Newspapers appeared first, for they were cheap and sometimes could be gotten for free, if I hung out long enough with the vendor on our street. Then at some point magazines and comics became a thing for the boys. Most wouldn't let me borrow their collection, but once in a while I could trade in a few favors—chores, food, spare change—to browse through the pages in installments. Finally, when my reading skills improved enough that I no longer had to rely on pictures, I was able to borrow books from the school library. This coincided with the time when I grew to appreciate language. Certain words stood out to me. Even if I didn't necessarily know their meaning, their sounds enticed me to consider them as keepsakes. But I've already told you about that episode of my life.

I had been living at the boarding school for about five years and had mostly lost touch with my father, when, just before school was about to start up again, he appeared out of the blue and asked if he could take me to breakfast. You can imagine that I didn't want to talk to him. I didn't even want to be seen talking to him, because then I'd have to answer pesky questions from the other boys, who might even tease me. But my father insisted. I thought perhaps it might be better, if he was going to be such a pain about it, to be anywhere else *but* at the boarding school, so we went to a café by the park.

That was when he started to tell me his conversion story.

"Do you want to know what I did to Ka Noel?" he asked.

I just sat there staring at him, sipping on my cappuccino. I'd resolved not to talk to him, no matter how much he bribed me with food and drink. In lieu of a response I just sipped louder.

"Well, I didn't kill him," he said. He sighed, as if by saying those words he had forever relinquished that right.

It was too much for me to take—the magic egg and the flashing knife—all told by a father I had come to detest, who had grown older since I'd last seen him, his hair and beard like unkempt shrubbery.

"Of course you didn't," I said, unable to resist. "You don't have the guts."

He seemed unmoved. But I could tell from the way his blinking slowed that it had affected him internally, and the quiver of his lips told me that he was experiencing some pain, like a variant of the five stages of grief compressed into a few seconds. Finally he smiled that stupid smile.

Because I guess he had been victorious, in a way, by making me talk. I vowed not to let him have the pleasure again. For the rest of that morning, I just listened.

He did not kill him. He did more than not kill him. He forgave him. And at once, my father said, a great weight was lifted off of him—the weight he'd been carrying since my mother died.

Ka Noel invited him to stay for supper. It was Begnas, a ritual for a good harvest, and the villagers had brought chickens and a wild boar to slaughter. Around the fire, dancers swayed with their arms outstretched like birds. Instruments that sounded like kulintang maintained the same metallic riffs, shifting in tempo only to match the dancers' feet. My father began to shiver, so he moved closer to the fire. Ka Noel sat next to him and offered him a cup of basi. All night long they drank and chewed their way through the tough boar meat, and when the boar was all gone they ate the chicken, and when the chicken was all gone they improvised and grilled some monitor lizard, and when that, too, was all gone they moved to the civet, and when the civet was all gone they caught some frogs, on and on until my father stopped asking what they were eating or drinking. At some point, when the orange of the flames turned red, Ka Noel brought out two carved mahogany sticks. He brandished them near the fire with their ends pointing up—as if displaying a scroll without the parchment—and then he began to talk, my father said, Ka Noel began talking to the fire.

He took three questions from the villagers that night. Each time he'd pause before he spoke to the fire in a chanting drawl. In turn, the fire would respond by bending to one side or the other, or flickering even if there was no wind. Ka Noel would then interpret these signs for the questioner. The first question was about a young girl's pregnancy: What gender would the baby be? The fire flickered and Ka Noel said it was hard to tell. Somebody joked that perhaps the kid would also grow up confused about being a boy or a girl. The second question was about harvest, and Ka Noel said there would be enough rain, not too much but not too little, so they could anticipate an ordinary year. Finally, the third question was about their upcoming raid on a food distribution warehouse.

Judging by the men's faces, this question seemed to have broken an unspoken rule. Nevertheless, Ka Noel went along and passed on the question to the fire. It would be a success, he said. A hard-fought one, but still a success. The men cheered. Ka Noel looked exhausted afterward, as if talking to the fire had drained all his energy. But just as he seemed about to retire, he pointed at my father.

"This is your chance," Ka Noel said. "We don't usually allow an outsider, but I'll make an exception for you. Because of what you have gone through."

My father said he didn't even hesitate, for there was only one thing he'd always wanted to know. Up toward the stars he addressed his question: Is she happy?

Ka Noel lifted his two sticks for the last time that night and waited for an answer. The fire leaned to the left, then to the right, before settling back to the left. Ka Noel whispered to the fire and waited a moment to see if it would change its mind. But it didn't.

"Brother," he said, "I'm afraid the answer is no."

My father stayed for a few more days in Ka Noel's village. As tired as he was from his travels that first night, he could find no sleep. The crickets abused the thick mountain air to carry their coded messages, and the damp ground seeped through cracks on the earthen wall of the hut. The blankets that the villagers had lent him provided some warmth. But every time he was about to fall asleep, my father thought of the fire. How it had leaned to one side and then the other. How it reminded him of the way his wife, when ordering off a menu, would rest her chin on the well of her palm and lean this way, then that way, before making a decision.

The next morning, my father ventured out on his own. He found a dry creek to use as a trailway and trusted in its contours to lead him somewhere, anywhere. A bamboo trunk that had been last year's flotsam lay on the ground. He skinned it for a walking rod and for protection. The sun was already directly above, but the cool breeze coated my father from the heat. Only when he brushed against some amor seco and scratched his leg did he realize that his skin had burned all over. He sought shelter in the trees. There, the grass gave way to decaying wood. Fungi and ferns grew in a pattern, rarely side by side but alternating, growing bigger and bigger as the canopy expanded overhead. Wherever light penetrated, the mist created diagonals that seemed to be infused with both the fantastical and the diabolical. Shadows lurked in the dark. Not since he was a child reading Aesop's fables, my father said, had he felt such a sense of fairy-tale wonder. That sense of wonder would turn into something more indigenous, no less magical, for as soon as he came out to a clearing, he found himself at a hill surrounded by rice terraces. So vast were the terraces carved into the mountainside that my father felt as if the smallest movement would cause him to stumble, the gravity created by the bowl-like void between sky and terraces pulling him in.

And then, he told me, he realized why my mother had not been happy.

"It's because of you," he said.

I almost choked on my cappuccino, for I'd burst out laughing. My father seemed to have expected this. He waited as I retrieved a napkin to wipe off my nose and mouth. A few more giggles came out before I could stifle them. The waiter stopped by and asked if I wanted water. In between coughs, I said I was okay. He brought it to me anyway. I took a sip from the glass just to clear my throat and force my lips from curling up.

Throughout all this, my father remained stone-faced. And then, when I looked ready, he spoke again, in a kind of whisper.

"What I'd done to you."

That was it. The syntactic amendment that would change the meaning of his original sentence. It was the closest he'd come to asking for forgiveness. For being an awful father—my words, not his. To this day, I sometimes wonder if that was indeed his intention. Or was it perhaps to appease my dead mother, in case she'd haunt him and rob him of more sleep? Nor did my father ever clarify just how staring at some ancient staircase, no matter how majestic, provoked in him this particular epiphany. I guess that, in a way, he diverged from most conversion stories, which tend to spell out exactly what one saw and its symbolic equivalence. In any case, after I'd finished my drink, he drove me back to the boarding school, and I requested that he drop me off a good few meters away. As I closed the door of the car, he asked if he could take me out again someday.

"Someday," I said, feeling all too pleased with myself.

———

He arrived the next day shaved, combed, and cologned.

Look, maybe I was naïve to fall for his trick. Or maybe I enjoyed listening to his stories more than I'd ever admit. They were, after all, the kind of stories I liked at the time—the supernatural and the metaphysical. And, of course, they also had to do with my mother, whom I had essentially never met and whom my father, until then, had never deigned to discuss.

But I was mistaken. From then on we would just sit at the café, he with his Bible or *The Communist Manifesto*, and I with my coffee and pastry. In the beginning I thought it was part of his devious scheme to force me to talk. So I called his bluff. I asked the waiter for a newspaper while he refilled my cup. I also decided to order from the lunch menu, sampling the appetizers and then the main courses, more food than I could possibly eat, just to see my father's reaction. He'd always been a cheapskate. He'd often complained about restaurant markups, swearing that he could make the same dishes at home, never mind that he was barely ever at home.

This time, however, he never flinched. He even asked to see the dessert menu himself—my father, who disliked all things sweet and peripheral. When he went back to reading his books, he'd pause to pick up his pen, smile, and jot down a few notes on the side. I almost envied him his devotion. All right, I did envy him. So I brought my own books the following day—I'm guessing they were books such as *Dune* and *The Last Unicorn*—because I was so sure he'd object, saying I should read something more "substantial," and then I'd have a chance to defend myself by throwing the question back in his face—"But what, sir, *is* substantial?"—or perhaps I could annoy him by saying, "Do I look like I care?"

Instead, he just let me be.

Was it possible, I started to wonder, that he was truly a changed man? Was I just imagining things, or did he have a new aura about him—a certain calmness that seemed to unwrinkle him, to soften his forehead? The silence we shared became part of the expectation, and because of this, I forgot the game I had been playing. Now I kept silent because I was comfortable doing so. And he didn't tell any more stories, because, maybe, for him there simply were no more stories to be told.

Such was the state and ease of our interaction, or lack of it, that when he did break the silence one day by asking me if I was happy, I didn't know how to respond.

"I meant, are you happy," he said, "with where you are?"

"The boarding school?" I asked.

He nodded.

"Of course," I said, pausing to clear the cobwebs in my throat. "In fact, I'm very happy."

"Okay," he said. "Just curious."

It wasn't until he returned me to my room that I thought about his question more thoroughly. I went back and forth about whether he had deliberately planted an idea in my mind, using the Socratic method, to expose certain weaknesses. I concluded that I could not reach a conclusion, for lack of evidence. What was indisputable to me, meanwhile, was that I had exposed myself as a fool. Where a simple yes or no or even maybe would've sufficed, I'd chosen to say that I was "very" happy. And that, in turn, could mean only one thing: that I was terribly lonely.

I grabbed my towel and headed for the showers, promising myself that I would never again let my father think that I hated my life. You know, I had developed this whole mental system when I was little that allowed me to enter parallel universes through the power of words. I discovered early on, during those days when I was frequently left at home, that if you don't have a choice in a particular matter, complaining only makes it worse. Hell exists only for those capable of imagining it. "Conditioning," I think, is what the experts call it nowadays. Back then, it was merely mumbling to oneself.

"I'm alive and I'm happy," I said, as I lathered on some shampoo. "I am thankful for the roof above my head and the food on the table." I rubbed soap on my chest. "I am blessed, and must remember there are others not so lucky." I moved to wash my legs and feet. Just as I was about to stoop down, I heard a plopping noise behind me. I thought that perhaps I had dropped something. But it had sounded wet, like meat being slapped on a chopping board.

Then I cried.

Whoever said that boys will be boys needs to be locked up in a dank shower stall with his towel taken away from him. He needs to grapple with the image of a dead rat, pregnant, the seam of its belly half open to reveal the little pink maggots wriggling inside, unable to escape their mother's bruised body, and then he needs to tell me with a straight face whether boys should be boys, or wouldn't they be better off as men?

———

I waited for my father's arrival the next morning. I knew him from his footsteps because he always struck his heel on the upswing. His soles always wore off quicker than the rest of his shoe. But I was wrong about him. Because the man who knocked on my door that day did not tap his heel anymore. He walked with a confident stride. And that, more than anything else, proved to me that he was a changed man.

"Take me home," I begged.

"I haven't told you," he said. "But I've sold our house."

"Take me with you."

"Come live with me, then," he said. "Up in the mountains."

———

Milo came by again just as I was about to tell you my experience living in the mountains of Zambales. He said I had a visitor.

The truth: I was somewhat petrified, because I couldn't imagine who it was that might pay me a visit. I didn't exactly part on good terms with Manang Dionisia the last time she was here, when she accused me of being a coward. I was a bit apprehensive, then, because if it wasn't her, I imagined it could mean only one thing. Even though I knew Manang Dionisia to be highly virtuous, I was afraid her loyalty to her employer might supersede our friendship. And I couldn't blame her, really. People like us don't have the luxury of keeping each other's secrets.

But Milo had played a trick on me, that naughty boy. The "visitor" turned out to be none other than my doctor, or rather, the doctor assigned to my case. He was here to discuss the results of my urine test, the details of which I will not bore you with. The only thing you need to know is that I've suffered complications from surgery, which might require me to undergo some kind of dialysis—the doctor hasn't decided yet. And I'm telling you this only to save you a world of pain later. Because I'm sorry to say that you are inheriting from me, as I have inherited from my father, a pair of weak kidneys. But you are healthy, I hope, so you should take care of yourself while you still can.

There is another thing to which I must confess.

After Milo and the doctor left, I heard the clanging of silverware against ceramic coming from a few beds down the hall. We are separated here by thin plywood walls, but I could still make out some of the conversations from one of the patients who gets real visitors. His family comes to have dinner with him every weekend. They talk about the most mundane things, about the TV show he likes to watch, or whether he needs extra pillows for his bed. Sometimes, when he's feeling well enough, they talk about the prospect of him going back to school. It's really tempting for me to put myself in his place. And for a second I did wonder what it would've been like if you and your mother were here to visit me. What would we talk about? What kind of meal would we share? But this is too much of a good thing even to imagine.

Instead, I tried to think of what it must be like for you there, with your mother and her partner. I imagined the three of you sitting around a wooden table, soft, warm light pouring in from above, not the stark fluorescent we have here. You mother says something about how she's messed up the chicken, that she should've put it into the oven much earlier but completely forgot. She's always been very humble about her skills, you know, whatever they may be. Anyway, right after that, there's a man's voice, calm and reassuring, telling her that in his opinion the chicken has actually been cooked to perfection, not one minute over or under. He also calls her "my dear" not a few times. "My dear," he says, "you know you could open your own restaurant someday," and that makes your mother blush.

I'd be lying right now if I said that I wasn't jealous. I'd also be lying if I said it was the first time I imagined that scene. In fact, it's always the same dinner, the same soft lighting and the same roasted chicken. The man who has replaced me always cracks the same corny joke. But it doesn't matter. Because, deep down, I know that he's a good man. Between the two of us, in fact, he's the better sort of man. He has made her quite happy. And perhaps, in him, you've finally found yourself a good father.

4

WE WERE ON the MacArthur Highway, having already passed the San Miguel Brewery and crossed a few rivers along old bridges, when I heard the passenger window at the back being rolled down.

"Feeling hot, ma'am?" I asked.

"Just want to take in some fresh air," Mrs. Aquino said.

But fresh it was not. Although the tall buildings had receded, we had yet to escape the smog of Manila. Industrial chimney stacks loomed large like half-used cigarette packs on the horizon. I was going to ask Mrs. Aquino if she was feeling okay when I saw her wince. She looked pale, and the hand propping up her forehead told me everything I needed to know.

"I'm stopping here, ma'am."

"Don't," she said. "Just a little motion sickness. It'll go away."

"I'm stopping," I said. "Fuel's running low."

There was traffic as soon as we entered Malolos. Then I remembered it was Independence Day, and that a parade must just be starting, which would eventually make its way to Barasoain Church. This whole town is steeped in history, having been the birthplace of the Philippine Revolution. But all I wanted that morning was a gas station, and an excuse for Mrs. Aquino to catch her breath.

At the very first sight of a Caltex I pulled over and instantly forgot that the Crown's fuel tank was on the opposite side. I had to reverse and make a three-point turn. I was afraid this would make Mrs. Aquino even dizzier, so I drove very slowly, and the gas attendant must've thought I was a novice driver. After telling him to fill up the tank, I popped the hood open and read all the gauges out loud. This seemed to convince the attendant that I was no amateur, because, to my relief, he finally looked away.

Just as I was about to fill up the radiator fluid, I thought I saw a shadow emerge from the car and wobble into the convenience store. I quickly screwed the cap back on. When I checked, Mrs. Aquino had indeed disappeared from the backseat.

———

Inside the store, I rushed to find the bathroom. The ladies' room was locked but I could hear a faint sound. It was just as I had worried.

Someone was throwing up, or trying to throw up. I wanted to knock but thought better of it. Instead, I went to the cashier and asked for some medicine and a bottle of water. Not long after, Mrs. Aquino came out. I took her by the arm and helped her to the car before she could protest.

"I'm okay, Lito," she said.

But I insisted that she take the pill to help with her nausea. Her hand trembled as she drank. She managed a smile and said that, really, she was beginning to feel better. She didn't want us to waste any more precious time.

"All right, ma'am," I said.

Back at the car, as I fastened my seat belt, the gas attendant came over with the bill. Mrs. Aquino threw me her handbag and told me to look for her wallet.

"Excuse me," the attendant said. "But isn't that Mrs.—"

"No," I interrupted. "I'm afraid you're mistaken."

In the heat of the moment, I hadn't realized how exposed Mrs. Aquino had been. I told myself I had to do a better job of keeping her safe. The attendant looked disappointed.

I combed through the handbag in search of her wallet. It wasn't the first time I'd done this, by the way, but I knew Mrs. Aquino as a tidy woman, and that day the contents of her bag were a mess: sets of spare keys, rolled-up paper, receipts, sticky notes, a hairbrush, a compact mirror, an eyeglasses case, even what looked like half-eaten bread wrapped in plastic. Finally, I found the wallet.

"She sure looked like her," the gas attendant said, giving me the change.

"She gets that often," I said. "But you really think a president would be riding in an old piece of junk like this?"

"I guess not," he said. "You're right. Anyway, I think the real one's actually a little fatter."

"Right," I said, and thanked him. I closed the window to engage the full protection of the tint.

"Sorry about that, ma'am," I said.

"Don't worry," she said. "I rather took it as a compliment." I smiled, glad that she seemed to be back in good spirits.

As I was putting the wallet back in its place, something caught my eye. Wedged between the eyeglasses case and the hairbrush was a pink envelope—the baronial envelope Mrs. Aquino had read from this morning in the sunroom. I'd like to think that what I did next came from a sense of duty. I peeked, because I'd wanted to make sure that we were really headed to the right place—in case Mrs. Aquino had, you know, made a mistake. What I had not expected to see, however, at least not in my lifetime, was the sender's name right above the address of Baguio City.

Written in elegant handwritten script was the name

Imelda Marcos

———

Whatever in the world Mrs. Aquino has planned to do with Imelda Marcos is none of my business, I told myself. Not only was Mrs. Aquino an adult—she was my boss, my provider, and, lest I ever forget, a woman whose very face would likely grace the currency in this country someday. And who was I but a lowly driver, a man whose existence nobody would remember—if they'd even known I existed in the first place?

The medicine seemed to have taken its full effect on Mrs. Aquino. She slept with her head leaning against the window. The back of her palm served to buffer any shakes from the occasional potholes. We were then going rather slowly, as the road had narrowed quite a bit as it led to a set of humpbacked bridges. Flame trees on both sides covered the highway, slowly revealing the view ahead as if they were stage curtains being pulled to the sides.

I turned on the radio, which was preset to the classical station. Together with the wonderful scenery, the music somehow calmed me down. It reminded me of the pleasures of driving. No other profession allows so much access to both the city and the countryside. As I sat there with my hands effortlessly draped over the steering wheel, the gentle breeze of the air conditioner against my face, it struck me that I was still on my employer's time. I was using her vehicle and fuel, too, listening to Beethoven and Mozart, getting to do what doctors and lawyers and other educated types work so hard for all week long, hoping to experience on their vacation days a magical moment just like this one.

After passing over the last bridge, the radio signal got a little worse, so I switched it off. Rather than let it ruin my mood, I enjoyed the quiet solitude. I couldn't imagine another job with so much free time to meditate. This—the driver's seat—was not just my workplace; it was also my study. It was where, over the years, I came up with all kinds of ideas, some nonsensical, about history and people and language. And even if most of these would probably prove useless and destined only to follow me into my grave, at least I can say that I've lived a life of pondering many questions that were important to me—questions such as "Are we really alone in the universe?," "Does God exist?," "What is the best meal to have if you know you are about to die?," "And what happens afterward?," "What is the one thing I would change if I could travel back in time?"

Yes, some of these questions are routinely passed around between bouts of a drinking game. But ask yourself, how many people do you think have given them serious consideration? How many have taken the time, plumbing the depths of their souls for answers, and possibly concluded that they've only scratched the surface of the Truth? How many do you think could honestly admit to not knowing?

———————

The northerly route was one I had traveled many times before—when Mrs. Aquino used to live in Tarlac with her husband, and later on, when I'd visited my own father just a few towns past the Aquinos' old house.

Even with eyes closed, I think I could manage to pinpoint my exact location just by smelling the change in the air.

In Meycauayan, for example, the acidic stench of the tanneries was unmistakable. Then, in Malolos, the nose got a reprieve, as well as a treat in the form of the sweet fragrance of sugar and margarine wafting from the pastry shops, where the traditional ensaymada recipes date all the way back to the Spaniards. Finally, as we crossed the Angat River, the salty breeze told me I was entering Pampanga—a region with its own language and rich culinary heritage. The road was mostly surrounded by rice fields, though I was once told that the whole area used to be a swamp.

Do you know that, out of all the five senses, nothing evokes memory more intensely than the sense of smell? Hearing, I think, is a close second, especially when one listens to a song linked to a particular period in one's life. Most songs are rather trapped in the era in which they became popular—think of boogie and disco. Taste, too, can bring back the past, which is why food from one's childhood is particularly precious. But food can be hard to re-create, requiring specific ingredients, oils, aromas. And so we always return to this, the sense of smell.

The Toyota Crown, built in 1992 and bought the same year,

had its own set of smells. Mrs. Aquino had just retired back then and needed a private car. She'd asked me for some recommendations, and because I'd gotten used to driving the government-issued Mercedes, I'd suggested the latest model from the same maker.

"Is it durable?" she'd asked.

"Yes," I'd said, "but rather expensive."

"What about something more affordable but built to last?"

After the purchase, the media fussed over the symbolism behind her choice. They said it was a smart move, to draw a contrast between the simplicity of the Aquinos versus the lavishness of the Marcoses. But I can tell you from my own experience that even before she became president, it was never Mrs. Aquino's style to be flashy. I'm saying this more as a statement of fact than of judgment: she just couldn't help but be cheap—unless, of course, she was spending on someone else, such as her kids or grandkids.

As I was saying, the Crown had a certain smell to it and still does up to this day.

There's a funny story as to why. One Sunday morning after church, we were driving her grandkids home together, and Mrs. Aquino, as was her tendency in those days, had given each of the siblings some candies. I think it was Migs or Nina who commented on the smell of the new car. "*Lola*, why does it stink here so much?" So the next week I made sure to hang up a couple of those pine air fresheners. But it did no good, because those grandkids of hers, since they were children, had some amazing noses. They not only continued to dislike the car smell, but also came to hate the little pine trees. I didn't blame them, though, because those things can be pretty noxious to a sensitive person.

Eventually the new plastic smell disappeared and I threw

away the fresheners, but it wasn't long before Mrs. Aquino mentioned that another scent had emerged. It was familiar, earthy, and not unpleasant. After investigating, I discovered that there were brown clumps clinging to the carpet underneath the passenger seats. I admit I was curious enough to take a swipe and a sniff—and even a taste of it—to confirm my suspicion. Whether by accident or on purpose, the grandkids had dropped their chocolates on the floor. I washed the carpet as thoroughly as I could, but by then I think the cacao oil had already penetrated deep inside. Over the years, the oils would only evolve. They'd become more and more potent and complex, so if someone were to angle the air conditioner just right, I believe he'd still be able to summon the spirit of that chocolate. And those grandkids of hers, who've now all grown older and hopefully wiser, would reappear in the backseat.

It is a curse—or a blessing, depending on one's mood and circumstances at the time—that after working closely with a family, one inevitably develops feelings for that family. It's a blessing, I suppose, to adopt new kin, especially if one's initial set was not so kind. It's instructive to see how other human beings are brought up, how they interact, so one comes to a fuller appreciation of one's own upbringing. But it's also a curse, because no matter how close the relationship becomes, one always knows deep down that one will never truly be part of that other family.

Her kids call me "kuya" or "tito," and the grandkids call me "manong." They use "po" and "opo," the honorifics reserved for elders. I, on the other hand, refer to most of them as "sir" or "ma'am"—even the grandkids, as soon as they begin to look like adults. It is all very gracious, really, all very Filipino, and perhaps, to outsiders, all very strange.

This morning, I was able to get up with the sun, like I used to do. I think I'm feeling somewhat better, somewhat happier, though still not strong enough to take my daily walks. So I decided I'd check out the box of books I brought with me from home. Not incidentally, I chose the one titled *Today's Revolution: Democracy*. It was written by Ferdinand Marcos in the seventies. I've always been curious to read it, you know. But, given who my employers were back then, I suppose you'd understand why I kept putting it off for another day. Well, now I have little to lose or gain, so that day seems finally to have come.

Milo saw me as he was making his rounds. He saw the book cover, but I sensed he didn't want to say anything at first. So I goaded him.

"Tell me I'm reading the devil's bible."

"I never said that, sir. I didn't even know he wrote a book."

"Several, in fact. All having to do with his theories on democracy, if that surprises you."

Milo adjusted the curtains to let in more light. He looked quite young and radiant—not a spot or wrinkle on his face. I say this only because I was contemplating how much he might know about the Marcoses and that whole saga. Probably not much.

"How is it so far, sir?" He sat next to me and rolled up my sleeve. He inserted the Velcro cuff on my arm and started taking my blood pressure.

"Very lucid and convincing," I said. "It boggles the mind."

"Let me know if it's too tight."

"He's basically making the case for martial law, calling it a revolution from within. He's out to reform not just the system but the very core of society. He thinks we were stunted because of colonialism."

"Just relax your hand for a minute, sir."

"He says the Filipinos use politicians like lords in the feudal age, asking for personal favors, a sack of rice or maybe some chickens. Or to put our family members in jobs that pay well. We elect the people who can deliver those things. We have a democracy only in name, he says, but it usually serves just a few people, not the majority."

"That sounds like some of my relatives you're talking about, sir," Milo said. I let out a laugh. "I'm not joking, sir. I think it has to do with our tribalism. We look out only for our own kind. The relatives I mentioned, they'll vote for any Ilocano who runs for office."

"Yeah? And what do you think of the Marcoses and their return to power?"

Milo hesitated before putting down his stethoscope. "To be honest, sir, I didn't vote. I've never voted. I really don't care about politics. I know it sounds common, but whoever's in charge doesn't make my life any better. In fact, I've heard of good friendships getting broken over talk of politics. So if you'll excuse me, sir," he said, unrolling my sleeve.

What Milo said is more or less what Mr. Marcos himself writes in his book. I haven't finished reading it yet, of course, but so far I'm impressed with the depth of his analysis. He traces the roots of democracy all the way back to Athens, with Plato, and then to the Founding Fathers in America, as well as our very own Ilustrados fighting for freedom. Part of Mr. Marcos's argument is that people have to adopt democracy on their own terms, when the time is ripe. In the case of the Philippines, American-style democracy was forced upon us. It was used by a few at the top to control the masses, who were too poor and too hungry at the time, says Mr. Marcos, to appreciate the concept.

I disagree, however, with what Milo said—the popular belief that it doesn't matter who's in charge during a given period. That is a dangerously cynical view to take, and not always an accurate one. While it may be true that one good person can do little to change a broken system, it's also true that one negligent individual can cause a world of harm. After all, isn't the correct solution often harder to arrive at than several wrong ones? Anybody attempting to solve a math problem could tell you that. Now imagine if we're talking about a hypothetical leader who is not just negligent, but malicious and selfish, too. What if this leader is wrangling not with math problems but actual human lives?

I'm sorry to be stepping onto my soapbox for a minute. But whatever they may say about Mrs. Aquino, whatever the disappointments and failures of her time in office—which, I admit, were not few—whatever the incompetency of her cabinet or indeed of herself, they cannot take away the fact that she was an honest woman, as honest as she tried to be in her service. I have lived my whole adult life as a witness to this. And it is among the few things on which I would gladly stake my honor.

Speaking of honesty, I remember a debate I once had, many years ago, with Manang Dionisia. It concerned a maid who had been laid off by the family. I was outside washing the car, having just driven Mrs. Aquino and her kids home for dinner. Manang Dionisia came to tell me the news.

"Lillian's no longer with us," she said. "I caught her stealing."

I said I was very sorry to hear it.

"Sorry? You should be glad she's not around anymore."

"I guess I'm sorry I didn't get to know her enough. I can't imagine what kind of desperation drove her to do such a thing."

"There was no desperation," Manang Dionisia said. "All she needed was provided for her right here."

"Could there have been a sick relative, perhaps?"

"Oh, it's always that excuse, isn't it? Then she should've just told us. Madam could have helped her."

"You know it's not always easy," I said, "to come out with such things."

"Then I'm sorry she has to suffer the consequences."

"Maybe you're right," I said, then sighed.

"I don't like being right," she said. "I wish it didn't happen at all. It's not easy for me, either, you know, depriving someone of a livelihood."

I nodded.

"Madam gave her some parting money and I walked her to the terminal. She rode the first bus to Olongapo."

"She should make it before midnight," I said. "What an ordeal."

"At least it's over and done with," she said. "Now to look for a replacement. And hopefully, this time, someone who knows the boundary between work and personal life."

We left it at that, for the meantime, because Manang Dionisia went back inside to clear the table and I went to rinse the suds off the car.

What she had said, however, unsettled me. I thought she was taking rather too many liberties in her assumptions about the kind of person the maid was. After all, very few of us could easily construct the boundary that Manang Dionisia had described. She herself could be woken up in the middle of the night if the Aquinos needed something urgent. And I, too, could be called upon on holidays and be expected to drop any previous plans. What "personal life," then, did we truly have?

The next morning, as I went to fetch the car keys from the kitchen, I told Manang Dionisia I thought she had been wrong.

"Are you okay, Lito?"

"I meant about last night." I explained that I'd reconsidered the issue and had wanted, out of a desire for openness and fairness, to say that none of us actually knew the maid's true situation. If we'd been in her shoes, I said, perhaps we'd have done the same thing.

"Only in your dreams," Manang Dionisia said. "I know what is right from what is wrong."

"But you have to admit that we both have much to lose."

"What are you saying?"

"Just that we shouldn't be too quick to judge, Manang. It's easy for the rich to be honest, you know. Not so much for us."

"What a load of crap," she said. "You either got it in you or you don't."

"You mean the fear of being caught?"

"Of doing the right thing! Now leave me alone, Lito," she said. "I have better things to do than philosophize with a deadhead."

Manang Dionisia's always resorted to name-calling, hasn't she?

And I was very young then, if not too feisty. I can see all of it now. Today, if asked why some people lie or cheat while others don't, I'd not focus on a person's wealth. I'm now convinced it has more to do with a person's ability to justify things, and, more important, his connection to reality. If he has a weak grasp on reality, refuses to see what is evident around him or what the preponderance of people is telling him, and instead persuades himself of a different version of events, he's more likely to steal or cheat, in my opinion. Because then won't he easily imagine his actions, his stealing or cheating, as something else altogether—perhaps something kinder? Unfortunately, it's been my experience that these people tend to be highly intelligent, and often have the gift not only to persuade themselves but also to persuade others of the truth of the lie.

In any case, the debate was moot, because not too long after, a replacement for the maid was found. She was from the same province as Manang Dionisia—who said the girl was penniless, but "from a family of good stock." We all watched as the girl glided her way in on the first day: confident yet unpretentious in her work; friendly yet circumspect. I can tell you that ever since that day, there was no one I know of who was more kind, more patient, who had more integrity in everything she did, down to the smallest details, than your mother.

Even I had to concede that Manang Dionisia had won that round.

We arrived before noon at Pampanga, a place that might be of some interest to you. You might be intrigued to know that Pampanga once held the largest American base outside your country. Unfortunately, you also know what happens when you put that many boys in one tiny neighborhood, far away from their homes.

Today, Pampanga has been transformed into a commercial village. Mrs. Aquino and I had just passed through the concrete gates that used to be part of the air base, when white sand—or what looked like white sand, at least—found its way to our windshield. It was actually lahar from the eruption of Mount Pinatubo, more than twenty years ago. The land has an amazing capacity for memory.

I admit that at the time, more than anything else, I might have been thinking of sisig—crispy pork bits doused with key lime and a runny egg, served on a sizzling plate. I don't believe you would have tried this yet? Or of buro: vegetable stew in fermented rice paste, or of bringhe, a kind of paella cooked in coconut milk. By then my stomach had started to growl. I'd woken up so early that morning that I hadn't had the chance to take in anything but a cup of coffee. I would also never have been bold enough to suggest to Mrs. Aquino that we stop for lunch. So instead I tried the radio to see if I could pick up any new station. But there were none.

"Are you hungry, Lito?" Mrs. Aquino asked.

"I'm fine, ma'am," I said. "We're making good progress. Nearly halfway there."

"Yes, I know. Are you sure you're okay?"

"Yes, ma'am. Yourself?"

"I'm all right."

We slowed down for a traffic light, and some vendor selling sweet corn approached. He was pushing a wheelbarrow and
balancing a metal drum from which steam was oozing out. I
hesitated before waving him away. That was when my stomach
complained again.

"Lito, can you still turn around here?"

"Why's that, ma'am?"

"I thought I saw a few restaurants over on the other side," she
said. "Come to think of it, I might just be a little hungry."

I didn't suppose for a minute that Mrs. Aquino was hungry. I
knew that she did it for me. Likewise, I would've been so much
happier had we stopped at a local carinderia—the kind of mom-
and-pop food shack I like. Instead, when she asked where we
should eat, I suggested a drive-through, saying, "We'll save time
this way, ma'am." But her security was really at the top of my
mind.

Once we were in front of the menu board, Mrs. Aquino told
me I should order whatever I wanted.

"Just a hamburger."

"Come on, Lito."

"Okay, ma'am. A hamburger meal."

As I was closest to the microphone, I placed my order first.
Then I asked what she wanted.

"Hamburger, too."

"One hamburger sandwich," I said.

"No, Lito," she said. "I also want the meal."

I apologized and corrected the order.

"Large, please," Mrs. Aquino said.

"Make that a large," I said to the microphone.

"Will that be all, sir?" came the cashier.

"Yes," I said to Mrs. Aquino's simultaneous "No."

"Three more hamburgers, three french fries, and three peach mango pies," she said. "And do you still sell those kiddie meals?"

We ended up parking just outside the fast-food joint, as Mrs. Aquino insisted that I eat properly—she'd have none of that balancing-food-while-driving business. Naturally, I thanked her. I was working through my french fries while they were hot and crispy. I was trying to think of a discreet way of asking why she'd ordered so many items.

"It's great to see that you've regained your appetite, ma'am."

"Lito, I can't remember the last time I've eaten these things. I know they're unhealthy. But look at me."

I turned around to see two fries sticking out of her mouth. She grinned like a walrus. I smiled.

"I heard it can be good for the soul, ma'am."

"Then I propose we eat nothing but fast food for the rest of our lives."

"It does seem like that is your intention, ma'am."

"What do you mean? This?" She rummaged through her stash of plastic bags like a dragon counting her gold. "Dear, have you forgotten my episode this morning? My stomach's emptier than yours."

"Of course, ma'am. I'd just be careful, you know, about eating them all at once. If I were you."

"Oh, Lito. When did you become *so* serious?"

"Excuse me, ma'am?" I turned around once more.

"I said, when did you—" She burst out laughing as soon as she saw that I, too, had grown some tusks. I pushed the fries into my mouth.

"These aren't actually for me," Mrs. Aquino said. "I figured we might as well pass by the old house on the way to Baguio. We can get another bathroom break. We'll surprise Manang Dionisia."

"That's very kind of you, ma'am. I'm sure the little ones would enjoy the kiddie meals."

As if on cue, Mrs. Aquino's cell phone rang. But she was busy taking big bites out of her hamburger. It rang some more before it finally stopped.

We sat there in silence, or at least almost total silence. We spoke to each other in code—through a series of cola sips, burger munches, and loud belches—first from her, then, so as not to alienate her, also from me. I felt strangely connected, something I hadn't felt for a long time. When I asked, "Is everything still good, ma'am?" it suddenly occurred to me how similar *ma'am* sounded to *mom*, especially with our accent. I wondered if the origin of those two words had any connection. It was too close to have been a coincidence. And then I started wondering about that other thing.

"Ma'am, forgive me if it's not my place to ask. But do you mind telling me why we're going to Baguio?"

"I already did," she said, in between chews. "We're going to visit an old friend of mine."

"Imelda Marcos is an old friend, ma'am?"

Except for a brief pause, Mrs. Aquino didn't show any signs of surprise.

"Acquaintance," she said. "From a long, long time ago."

"I'm sorry, I didn't know that," I said.

"It's my fault," she said. "I guess now you're curious why we're going to her house."

"It's not my place, ma'am—"

"But you already know why, Lito."

Her sudden curtness flustered me. Then she asked for my food wrappers, because she said she was going out for the trash bin. I offered to take hers instead.

On the way back to the car, I kept asking myself if I really knew why we were off to see Imelda Marcos. Could it really be? But why now? What had changed? Something was not right, and it was making my stomach churn.

5

MY FATHER AND I lived in a small hut at the woodsy edge of Ka Noel's village, where some wild fowl roamed free. Whenever the sun rose, we heard the calling of roosters, followed by the angry barking of dogs chasing them down.

We arrived at the start of the monsoon season. If I'd thought the boarding school accommodations were shabby, clearly I'd lacked imagination. Because our hut had been unoccupied before we moved in, it was in serious need of repair. It swayed and creaked during the worst of a storm. Some slats in the ceiling were missing. Bird feathers and droppings told half of the story. Termite frass, gathered like piles of sesame seeds on the rafters and the flooring, told the other.

The closest outhouse was about a ten-minute walk toward the center of the village. Nobody used it but us. Most other huts shared toilets, with about four huts to one, but ours was too far out for any neighbors to join in. My father promised that he'd build us our own toilet as soon as the sky cleared up. He also promised a new bed, a closet, and a bookshelf, because we were using the shelf we had as a dresser. We wrapped our few books in cellophane and tucked them under our beds to protect them from the rain. But I'd also like to think that sleeping so close to books offered us some very interesting and vivid dreams.

When I look back on this time, what remains with me is how I went from almost never seeing my father to seeing nobody *but* my father. During the first few months, in particular, the monsoon cast a kind of shroud upon the whole village, and communal activities were few. The only times my father and I were invited to mingle fell on Sundays, when Ka Noel held mass inside a small basketball court. Under the tin-sheet awning, Ka Noel preached the gospel of Marx and Jesus.

You'd be surprised, actually, by how seamless the blending of the two ideologies turned out to be. Ka Noel spoke often about the blessedness of the poor, how they'd one day inherit the kingdoms of God *and* of man. He railed against the rich, especially the landowners, the bankers, the money changers. He even talked down the Church establishment all the way to Rome, saying that they were interested only in preserving their power. If that doesn't sound like Jesus on the Temple Mount preaching against the Pharisees, I don't know what does.

Marx's own hesitations about religion—or even condemnation of it—were glossed over in these sermons. I would find out about that only much later. Ka Noel seemed to pick and choose the things that suited him and his community, even drawing from some traditions long practiced by the local people. Still, I think it's fair to say that most of the tribes living around those parts, whether they were Communist or Christian or what have you, would've thought some of the things we did were strange. Nobody admitted it, but we in the village were, first and foremost, followers of Ka Noel.

I still remember my introduction to the Eucharist, which we also called Holy Communion—another term that conveniently united the two ideologies. In any case, after Ka Noel recited his homily, he received the three gifts in succession at the altar. This was accompanied by the sound of gongs. First he blessed the unleavened bread, breaking it into pieces on a plate. Then he lifted the wine and poured it into the chalice, in remembrance of Jesus on the night before he was crucified, at which point Ka Noel's assistant carried up a chicken by its neck. Ka Noel blessed this, too, proclaiming the sacrifice of the people and the consent of the land.

I always became very excited in the brief pause that followed. Would he do something like what my father had described with the glowing egg, or with the mahogany sticks by the campfire? What was Ka Noel going to do with the live chicken? But, other than the bird's brief struggle as the knife swiped its neck and blood dripped into the chalice, the act soon became mundane. The congregants lined up to take part in the sacrament. The congregants retook their seats. In a short while the whole thing was over.

There was one very good reason why we and the rest of the villagers loved attending mass every Sunday: It was here, after shaking Ka Noel's hand and getting his blessing, that we received our rations. With factory-like efficiency, the women sorted our supplies into baskets. They varied from week to week, but we could usually expect to see rice, cooking oil, eggs, cabbages, tomatoes, onions, and garlic. We'd also have dry goods like milk powder, coffee, sugar, salt, pepper, cans of sardines, candles, and matches. Sometimes packs of instant noodles appeared—those were especially prized. Other essentials, like soap and shampoo, were mostly traded. No money changed hands, of course. People bartered with meat from the animals they raised, firewood from clearing the forest, or sometimes they traded favors, like watching over children or cooking special dishes.

Since my father and I did not contribute to work in the beginning, we always received our basket with tails tucked firmly between our legs. I tell you, there was nothing quite like seeing the face of my father as he profusely thanked the women for supplies we'd taken for granted back home. His shame quickly spilled over to me, too, so that I'd bow my head as he muttered apologies, saying, "It's temporary, you know. My son and I are in the process of adjusting."

For the most part, the women were very generous and would wave away our excuses. Still, this did not tempt us to be sociable, and we always rushed off to our hut right afterward. And I could read it as plain as day on my father's face: each time he received the supplies, he vowed to return only when we could do so with dignity.

One Sunday, my father skipped mass because he said he wasn't feeling well. I made him some rice porridge and left it on the table so he'd have something to eat when he woke up. By the time I got to the basketball court, the villagers had already dispersed. I thought I might as well try my luck with the rations. There was only one woman tending to the supplies. Her lips were burnt red and her teeth stained from chewing betel. I'd never tried betel in my life, but from her expression I imagined it must've been very sour or bitter. She pretended not to see me. I greeted her.

"I'm closed," she said.

I explained my father's condition and said I was sorry for being late. I then pointed to the remaining baskets, which were still sitting on the floor next to her, filled to the brim. But Betel Lady wouldn't budge. Again she said she was closed. "Besides," she said, "these are for people who don't just stay home and sleep all day."

What could I do? I was just a teenager whose Adam's apple hadn't even popped. I shrugged off the insult and started on my way home.

"Just a minute," said a man's voice. "Come back."

It was Ka Noel, clad in his Sunday vestments, wrapping up a conversation with one of the villagers. I waited a few feet away from them, careful not to appear too eager or as though I were eavesdropping.

"Lito, right?" he said, approaching me. He took my hand with both of his but didn't shake it, just cupped it as though between a pair of clamshells. He always struck me as being taller face-to-face than when he stood on the pulpit. "How are you and your father?"

I said we were both doing fine. Immediately he sensed my hesitation. And I think that, if nothing else, that man had a gift for perception, because he led me right outside the door, so we could be alone. The way he did it, too, deserves some mention. If anyone saw us, I bet they wouldn't be able to tell if it was Ka Noel leading me out or if I was assisting him like I might my uncle. So slight was the pressure he placed on my hand that, years later, I still remember it as something like dancing.

In any case, I ended up telling him everything that day. About my father feeling sick. About the holes in the roof that we'd tried to stuff with banana leaves and stems. About the mosquitoes and insects and ants that came from every which way because the hut was pervious like a sieve. I even told him, rather shamelessly, about my bowel movements. How I had to hold it in sometimes because the outhouse was too far away and I was too afraid to venture out in the middle of the night.

He laughed at this last revelation—but a soft, almost embarrassed kind of laughter. Then he squeezed my hand and said he was very, very sorry because he had been too busy to personally see to us. He asked why we hadn't told him earlier about all our troubles. I said my father didn't want to be a nuisance.

"Well, next time, don't ever be afraid to tell me anything, anything at all."

He promised he was going to rectify the situation, and I thanked him. As we made our way back inside, Betel Lady saw us and quickly snapped to attention. On Ka Noel's prompting, she handed me not one basket, but two.

———

Later that same day, Ka Noel's men showed up at our hut, bringing with them some lumber and a plastic tarp and aluminum screen. My father let them in but turned to look at me. He seemed upset. Maybe it was because I'd left him in the dark about my conversation with Ka Noel. Or because I'd troubled the villagers and, in the process, proved the utter ineptitude of us lowlanders.

I hurried off to boil water for coffee and to prepare some food. I counted at least five men, though I figured that, after several hours of work, their appetites might easily match those of many more. So I used up all the instant noodles we'd been saving, only to realize, rather too late, that this might worsen my father's mood. When I went to consult him, however, I was surprised to see him turned into one of the workers, sawing his way through a hardwood plank.

There is pleasure to be derived in watching men who are good with their hands. Even if it made me wonder how my life had turned out this way. It made me a little sore with my father, because carpentry seemed exactly like something I should've learned from him while I was growing up, just as he probably learned it from his own father.

In no time the hut was sealed from top to bottom. Gone were the leaky roof and the holes in the floor. The wood paneling had been re-varnished. The windows were patched with new screens. The men had eaten up all the food and drink, then left. The place, though repaired, was a mess.

I started sweeping. My father, impressed at my diligence, picked up the mop. We worked mostly in silence but in tandem. After the dirt was cleared, we decided to wax the floor. Then, while waiting for it to dry, we washed the mugs and dishes. After that we went back to our knees, scrubbing the floor with coconut husks until it reflected our faces and our feet were numb.

Finally, he looked at me and said, "Son, I think we did okay here, don't you?"

"I think we did," I said. And then, as if someone or something had possessed me, I asked my father about his sickness.

He touched his forehead and said, "Gone. Apparently what I

needed was some hard work." When I didn't respond, he asked, "What's wrong?"

I pointed at the black smudges all over his face. He began wiping himself with his shirt.

"I stink," I said, smelling my armpits. "But I'm too tired to go out to the well. I miss running water."

For a moment we just sat there, staring at our handsomely restored hut, listening to the start of the pitter-patter on the thatched roof and on the plastic tarp. It was good to know we were now protected from the elements.

Then my father stood up and took off his clothes.

Before I could ask what he was doing, he had disappeared out the door. A spray of rain and cold breeze blew in and stung my face.

"Come on outside," I heard him shout.

"You're crazy!" I shouted back.

But as I went to close the door, I thought, Just how bad could it be? I took off my own clothes.

I had, of course, seen bare-skinned boys at the boarding school. But it's altogether a different story to witness for the first time the nakedness of one's parent. The pine trees and the mist surrounding us did help. They not only provided cover from prying eyes, but also made me feel like a part of nature. After all, we don't feel ashamed on behalf of the sheep and goats and cows in the field, do we? It's an illusion to think that we should be any different from them. This fact slowly settled in me, and soon I ceased to feel uncomfortable about my father's body. I thought something rather primitive and profound was happening as we passed the soap and helped lather each other's backs in the middle of a forest. It felt as if I was getting to discover something true about myself that I had long ago lost.

———

Having our hut fixed meant we were able to sleep more soundly that night and the many nights after. Having slept more soundly meant we were able to wake up earlier in the morning. And waking up early in the morning infused us with a new sense of hope.

One day, while I was returning from the well with our water, I noticed a plump honeydew melon sitting near the dirt path. Whether it had recently sprouted or I'd just been too preoccupied to notice, I wasn't sure. Likely it was the latter. Because when I followed the vine to its source, I found an entire vegetable garden I'd also never noticed before. The garden had a wide variety of produce, all the kinds I missed—snow cabbage, winged beans, string beans, ladyfingers, bell peppers, eggplant—along with other greens I couldn't identify back then.

"What do you want?" a woman's voice called out.

When she emerged from her hut, I saw that it was the same woman from the Sunday supply store: Betel Lady. She hurried to block my passage, obviously thinking that I was there to steal. I took a step back.

"Your vegetables are looking very healthy. I'm just admiring them, ma'am," I said, and quickly added, "from afar, of course."

"Don't you 'ma'am' me," she said, folding the hem of her pants.

"Oh, I'm sorry, auntie."

"Don't 'auntie' me, either."

Not knowing how else to respond, I said, "I should probably be on my way. I didn't mean to be a bother."

"Vegetables don't grow by themselves," she said. "It takes a lot of hard work, that's how."

It could be that she was insulting me, insinuating that I wasn't up for any kind of work. But it also sounded as if she might be offering me an opening. In any case, I thanked her and picked up my bamboo pole, from either end of which a pail of water swayed.

I'd just walked a few feet from the garden when I had the thought that I had nothing to lose. So I turned around, and there she still was, glaring at me.

"Now what?" she said.

I almost stumbled at her gruffness. I held on to the pole for balance. I said, "It just so happens that . . . I collected too much water for our own use and I . . . I was curious if perhaps you might want some . . . for your plants."

"I don't," she said.

"Okay," I said, wondering how some people could be so mean. I prepared to leave as soon as possible and to never look back. But then she hissed at me, a long *pshhhhhhsssttt* sound, which turned out to be just a practical way of calling for someone's attention—common around those parts.

"The plants don't need watering, because of all the rain," she said. "But I sure do." She approached me, the bigness of her bones causing her to waddle like a duck. She tipped over one of my pails to splash water on her grimy feet and slippers, then again to wash her hands. "These days all my time is spent weeding and pruning or shooing away birds. Might not sound like much to you. But this is on top of everything else I do, like cooking and cleaning."

"I cook and clean at ours, too," I said.

"And?"

"And, this. Fetch water."

"And?"

She was starting to get on my nerves. And I think she felt it, too, because she let out a sigh.

"I'd do more if I could," I said. "I'd have a garden like yours, if I knew how."

"You might think you're still a boy," she said. "But here, boys your age go out to train and fight. That's why you don't see many of them around, in case you were wondering."

I nodded.

"Even during the monsoon they go out into the jungle. Picking up some skills, my husband likes to say. He and the others often come back muddy and I have to wash all their clothes. I'm not complaining. Just wish they'd have enough sense to train when it's drier, you know. But I guess you can't choose when to go to war."

"Guess not," I said.

"Between you and me—"

"Lito," I said.

"Lito, I'd rather the men stay here longer. Work's never-ending as it is, and I sure could use some help with the heavy lifting. It's just that they see it all as tedious and trivial business. Of course they'd rather be out running somewhere else. More exciting to shoot a gun, I suppose. Even I can see that."

"I've never touched a gun in my life," I said. "And I've no intention to."

"Anyway," she said. "There's some leftover pumpkin stew inside. Shame if it goes to waste."

Her name was Ka Anna. That was how she wanted to be addressed—as comrade, as equal, no matter our age and our differences. She told me to stop by again if I had the chance. She said she'd teach me things, if I wanted her to.

And so it was, over the following weeks, that I took her up on the offer. I learned how to grow a vegetable patch, how to choose a well-elevated site, how to create a system that allows rainwater to pass without flooding the vegetables. She gave me good, strong seeds and taught me how to plant each variety. She lent me a spade and a hoe and told me my likeliest enemies were not birds and insects but my neighbors, who were either envious or lazy or probably both. She said the sweetest thing in life, aside from swatting the behinds of such people, was to enjoy the fruit of your own labor. But remember, she said, and beware: you always reap what you sow.

While this went on, my father's role in the village would also be revealed to him. Not long after Ka Noel's men came to fix our hut, Ka Noel himself appeared one afternoon to pay us a visit.

"You're looking awfully good," he told me. I was outside tilling the soil on what would then become our own vegetable garden. I had slowly lost weight from all the work and had turned a shade darker. But I wasn't terribly conscious of this fact, as we didn't have a mirror inside the hut. What Ka Noel said, of course, made me smile.

He was wearing black slacks and a button-up shirt that day, as if he were reporting for office duty. He asked for my father and I told him to proceed inside. I continued with my own work.

After breaking up the plot of land, I dug up about a foot-long rectangular perimeter. I then opened the bag of earthworms that Ka Anna had given me and set them loose on the soil.

Ka Noel left rather unceremoniously afterward, though he did manage to say he was sorry for being in a rush. I waited until dinnertime to ask my father what they had discussed.

"Grown-up things," my father said. "Pass the salt."

"I am grown," I said. And as if to demonstrate, I held the salt hostage, taking my sweet time in sprinkling a generous amount on my milkfish before handing it to him. He shook his head.

"I'm prepping the soil for planting," I said. "As soon as it's ready, I'll throw in a few peanuts. Ka Anna said it shouldn't take long for them to mature. We should have some pods to harvest before the end of the year."

"It'd be nice to have garlic-fried peanuts again," he said.

I'd known, of course, that this was his favorite snack. "I like it here," I said. "I'm beginning to feel as if I finally belong. I have responsibilities, like a real adult. I'm not just fiddling around." Then, looking at him, I said, "Mother would be proud, I think. She'd be really happy."

That stopped his chewing. I couldn't tell if my father was angry or sad or pleased at what I had just said. Probably all of those things combined. "Lito, do you seriously mean that?"

I said I did.

"Okay," he said.

We proceeded to divide the last pieces of the fish, but instead of taking his share, my father laid it all on my plate. He said he was already full.

"Ka Noel wants me to go back," my father said, "to Moncada."

"What? Why?"

"He wants to put me in charge of collections there. He said I'd fit right in, and nobody would suspect anything. I haven't agreed to it yet. But I don't see how I can refuse. Still, I asked for some time to think about it."

As always when I felt distraught, I ate everything in sight. The fish. The cabbages and tomatoes. The bowl of rice. They almost spewed back out of my gut because of how fast I tried to put them in.

"Don't worry," my father said. "You can stay here. Ka Noel insisted he was going to personally look after you when I'm away."

"I don't want to," I said.

"But you said you like it here, don't you?"

It was cruel how my father turned my own words against me, though I don't think that was his intent. He just kept trying to console me, and himself, by saying, "It'll be okay, Lito. I won't be gone for any long stretches of time. It won't be so bad, I promise. It shouldn't be so bad."

It must be said, without a doubt, that those remaining days with my father up in the mountains of Zambales were truly some of the happiest in my life.

There was nothing particularly special to them. We woke up at the same time every day, ate the same breakfast, drank the same coffee. I then tended to my plants while he went off to see Ka Noel. At around noon, my father would return and I'd make sure we had something to eat. Again, nothing special here; lunch was a light affair of mostly stir-fried vegetables. My father couldn't stay long, because he said Ka Noel would become impatient. Ka Noel wanted him to read this and that document, or to introduce my father to certain people who would become key for his mission later. I don't know what the mission was, exactly. I collected only bits and pieces from what my father volunteered.

In the afternoons, I'd nap, followed by a lot of cleaning and washing—pots and pans, mostly, and the floor, which needed a lot of sweeping to keep the ants and bugs at bay. Once a week, I'd take our clothes and the bedsheets to a nearby creek. It was the easiest method, Ka Anna had taught me, since flowing water carries dirt and suds away. Otherwise, rinsing would be a difficult affair of slogging back and forth from the well. We'd be exhausted before we could even hang the laundry.

On good days, I'd pick up firewood from the forest, and if I was in the mood, I'd go foraging. There were lots of edible ferns to be found in the shade. Berries abounded, too. According to Ka Anna, there were two kinds—green and purple. The villagers used the green berries to sour up their soups. I heard they also used them as bait to catch cloud rats, which were a delicacy. The purple berries were reserved for rituals. It was believed that some local gods enjoyed them, and would favor the people who offered them this fruit. When the berries were ingested during rituals, it was said that the gods could reveal to people their past, present, and future.

Evenings, my father retired to the hut, and these were the best times. No longer saddled with chores or in a rush to go somewhere else, my father and I would sit by the kerosene lamp to read our books. He loved the biographies of famous men and women. It never failed to amaze me how thick those books were—just how much could one really pack into the telling of one's life? I preferred my mysteries and fantasies. Once, after seeing the face of a ghoul on the cover of my book, my father leaned forward to examine it. I quickly set it aside.

"Avoid the ficus," he said.

I had no idea what he was talking about.

"Strangler figs," he said. "The tree with overhanging roots."

"I know what a ficus is."

"Well, avoid it. There are plenty of spirits that live inside. If you're not careful, you might upset them. I was told that a boy and a girl disappeared in the woods last year."

"Since when did you start believing in ghosts?"

"Spirits," he said. "There's a difference."

"Okay," I said. I could almost hear in my father's voice that of Ka Noel, speaking from the pulpit.

"Take care of yourself," he said, "while I'm gone."

"Don't worry," I said. "I'll be sure to avoid the ficus." He didn't laugh.

"I almost forgot," my father said. "There's something I wanted to show you." He got up and went to his side of the bed, where he suddenly vanished, or so it seemed to me at first. He actually crawled all the way into the space beneath the mattress. He resurfaced, dragging out something rectangular and heavy and wrapped in what looked like old curtains. He dusted himself off and then told me to pull off the covers.

Inside was a small bookcase, made from wood of a deep red-brown grain I immediately recognized as narra, the noblest of the hardwood trees, so strong and dense it naturally resisted termites. He said that he'd worked on the bookcase at Ka Noel's, borrowing his tools and asking for any leftover lumber. But—my father insisted—he and he alone had put the whole thing together.

"A promise is a promise," he said. "But, Jesus, was it hard to keep a surprise from you. You and your constant sweeping."

I thanked him and hugged him. I had never before owned a bookcase, or any piece of furniture, for that matter. He didn't say much to me afterward, except that he'd try to bring me more books, so I could fill up the shelves. In turn, I didn't say much to him, either, except to tell him that I'd seriously miss him. Because I knew that with the gift, he had caused time to change, so that it would no longer flow effortlessly forward. With the gift, my father was putting an end to our carefree days up in the mountains.

The very next morning, he set out on his trek back to the lowlands. And as it turned out, our lives were never the same again.

———

Sometimes I wonder why I didn't insist on accompanying him, or even ask if I should. I wonder why I accepted my solitude again so willingly. Of course, part of it was Moncada itself, which reminded me of my childhood and all that entailed. It would have meant going back to the old life with my father, even if I thought he had changed. And part of it was the self-conditioning I was telling you about earlier. Trapped in a situation where I've little to no choice, my instinct is not to complain or resist, but to fantasize.

This kind of magical thinking was particularly easy in a place like the mountains. Somehow, when I was surrounded by the thick mist and cedar trees, it was tempting to believe that nothing had changed, and life would go on as we wanted it to, that I'd still wake with my father by my side and see him again before I went to sleep. I didn't know, or chose not to know, that his vow not to leave me for long stretches of time came out of compassion. Or, perhaps, my father was also engaged in his own version of magical thinking.

In any case, I was at Ka Anna's, helping her weed her vegetable garden, when Ka Noel materialized.

"I've been looking everywhere for you, Lito," he said.

I apologized before I could catch myself.

"Come," he told me. "We've no time to waste."

I must've looked to Ka Anna, because she answered on my behalf. "Ka Lito here has been so useful," she said. "I wouldn't know what to do without him these days." She lifted the hem of her pants and began rubbing her ankle.

"Really?" Ka Noel said. "I do hope and pray constantly for your recovery, sister. I know you're strong as a bull."

"A strong bull with a limp is hardly a bull at all," she said.

"Well, we shall always remember your sacrifice," he said. "Just as we remember the sacrifice of all the others."

"And what urgent thing might the reverend need Ka Lito for today?"

Ka Noel seemed to wince at the title. He said, "It's not what I need from Lito that has brought me today, sister. Rather, it's what he needs. We're to start his education. And the sooner we do it, the better."

"Of course," Ka Anna said. "How could I forget, the education."

I waited for her to say something more. But she just stared at her ankle, scratching, picking at an invisible scab. So I went to wash the dirt off my hands and feet. After I was done, Ka Anna grasped my wrist and said, "I'll keep an eye out for your return, okay?"

Then she let me go.

———

"How do you like your new bookcase?" Ka Noel asked me when we were alone on the path. His hut was on the other side of the mountain, as isolated as ours, except that his was perched higher, so he could keep watch for trespassers.

I said I was very pleased with it.

"You know, I helped with the base," he said. "It's very important for the base to be stable. Otherwise, the whole thing will lean over and collapse."

"Did you really?"

He nodded. "I don't think your father knows. He said he wanted to make it all by himself. He was very clear about it. So I fixed it only when he wasn't around. He's a proud father."

"I know," I said.

The clouds above us seemed to move with the same sluggishness as Ka Noel and I. But around us the trees became sparser, giving way to more and more huts, until I recognized the village center and the well in the middle of it. People greeted Ka Noel as they passed by.

"Can I ask you a question?" I said.

"If it's about your education," he said, "you better have more than just one question. I want an eager student." He laughed. "I can assure you, though, it'll be worth it in the end. You'll even thank me after."

"No," I said. "It's about Ka Anna. I didn't know she had an injury."

Ka Noel took a deep breath. "It happened some time ago. She was captured in a skirmish, along with her husband and other men."

"But the wounds have all healed?" I suggested.

"Yes and no," he said. "Not all wounds heal on the outside." Then, pointing to his head, he said, "You be careful with her, Lito. She's fragile."

"She seems fine to me," I said.

But Ka Noel's attention had already shifted elsewhere. He was staring at a burst of orange that the dark clouds had just uncovered. The bright color would slowly fill in the rest of the sky. Ka Noel whispered some kind of prayer, or maybe an incantation. Then he turned to me and smiled.

"We've reached the end of the monsoon."

6

WHAT DOES IT mean to forgive somebody? The question weighed heavily on my mind as I steered the Crown back to the highway. For why else would Mrs. Aquino, in her condition, take on such a difficult journey? And why would Imelda Marcos have written to her in the first place? Certainly the two of them weren't about to discuss the finer points of gardening.

Whereas before I could hide under the cloak of blissful ignorance, Mrs. Aquino's earlier statement—if not accusation—that I'd already known the reason for our trip woke me to the fact that I was a conspirator. Perhaps I just hadn't wanted to consider the consequences of a simple act like driving. But with every passing minute in the car, it seemed that I'd been left with little choice. The question had assumed existential, if not theological, dimensions.

Now, I'll be the first to admit that when it comes to theology, I am a fish out of water. I've never been a regular churchgoer. And among those few times I've tried, I've always found it hard to stay awake.

Presumably, it would be during the sermons that issues such as sin and forgiveness might arise. It is my own shortcoming, to be sure, that I often find the explanations too quick and pre-scriptive. Where I'd have liked to dwell on the questions a little longer, the answer—because it tends to be in the singular, doesn't it?—is almost always given at the end of the sermon. Still, as I drove Mrs. Aquino to Baguio, I regretted not having paid more attention during church.

But I had to remember that Mrs. Aquino, unlike me, *was* a woman of deep faith. She would've known the Bible's teachings by heart, and not only that, she would've tried to embody them. "Forgive us as we forgive those who trespass against us." I think that is from the Lord's Prayer. "Whosoever slaps you on the right cheek, turn the other also to him." That is Jesus, I believe, though from what chapter and verse I couldn't tell you. Was this journey, then, a kind of via dolorosa for Mrs. Aquino, an attempt for her to do the right thing for the very last time?

But what is forgiveness, anyway?

The simplicity of the question is staggering. All I could come up with back then was what forgiveness was not.

It is not, as some might think, the same thing as forgetting. One could forgive somebody without forgetting the transgres-sion. In fact, it's probably better to forgive *without* forgetting. That way, one might be less likely to put oneself into the same circum-stances, if at all possible.

Forgiveness is also not just a matter of saying, "I forgive you." Though that might be the first step, it seems to me that true forgiveness is letting go of the anger or the grudge. Now, that's a lot harder than just saying certain words. And sometimes it's not totally within our control. Our minds may want us to forgive somebody, but our hearts may not be willing to let go.

Forgiveness is also not about condoning. It's not saying that we've changed our minds about the act, or even that we feel its wrongness less intensely, because forgiveness is not exactly about rectifying the past. Indeed, there are some things that can never be rectified. Mrs. Aquino, try as she might, couldn't resurrect her husband from the grave. But she should still have been capable, if she was intent on it, of forgiving his killers.

———————

There is something you should know that might complicate this matter. The assassination of Mr. Aquino remains an unsolved mystery to this day. Officially, of course, it has been closed for many, many years. Now, I don't want to get too deep into this rabbit hole. There's plenty of information out there, as well as misinformation, which you can read and use to decide for yourself.

But I did, in fact, conduct a sort of thought experiment to see where people stand on the issue nowadays. And by *people*, I mean only Milo. By *nowadays*, I mean just this afternoon, when he came to deliver my food. Actually, I wouldn't go so far as to call it food. Sewer sludge would have been more accurate.

"Can I have some salt and pepper, please?" I asked Milo, while I poked the sliced carrots and broccoli around the plate with my fork. They were not even steamed, but boiled.

"I'm afraid not," he said. "We're controlling your sodium, sir. The doctor has decided to do your dialysis."

"Can you do me a favor and kill me now?" I said, setting the plate aside.

"Sir?" He propped a pillow at my back to help with the incline. "Don't worry," he said. "I know many patients with your condition who eventually recovered, after a few weeks."

"Unlike most patients," I said, "I don't have the patience."

"It can be cultivated, sir."

I smiled, and he smiled, too, and said, "Ah, you were joking, sir."

Baby steps, I thought.

"Can you keep me company for a while?" I asked. "I want you to play detective with me."

"I don't know what you mean," he said. "But I can stay here until the end of my shift, which is in half an hour."

"I'll try my best." I took a sip of water. "First question," I said. "Who do you think killed Ninoy Aquino?"

"Oh, we're back to politics," he said.

"Please? I promise it won't take long."

"Fine," he said. "If you promise you'll finish up all your veggies."

Like a child, I promised that I'd be good. "So, about my question."

"Didn't they say it was Ferdinand Marcos?"

"Well, he was certainly the most powerful man at the time. But an investigation right after the murder found that rogue military men were responsible."

"You're joking again, sir?"

"Why do you say that?" I asked.

"If the investigation happened when Marcos was the most

powerful man, like you said, how could you expect them to find him guilty?"

"Good point," I said. "But what if I tell you that during Mrs. Aquino's term, she also did an investigation. And the result was that they found the same military men to be guilty. Twenty-five of them were sentenced to life."

"And Mr. Marcos, sir?"

"In exile in Hawaii. But he wasn't made a suspect."

"I see," he said. "Let me think about this."

I put a stalk of broccoli into my mouth.

"How long after the assassination did this new investigation take place?"

"Three to six years, I think. Does it matter?"

"Well, it's more likely for a cover-up to have happened by then, sir."

"It's possible," I said. "But the fact that Mrs. Aquino's own probing didn't result in charging Mr. Marcos with the crime—isn't that saying something?"

"True," Milo said. "That's why I told you I don't like politics, sir. I don't understand it."

"All right," I said, adjusting my pillow. "Thanks for being a good sport. Enough questioning for now."

"Anyway, sir, I'm just a nurse," Milo said. "But I know that if we've just taken out some cancer cells from a patient, the last thing we'd ever want to do is to put those cancer cells back in."

Broccoli florets almost spurted out of my nose. I'd clearly misjudged the boy. "Did you just compare Mr. Marcos to cancer cells?"

"Oh no, I'm sorry, sir. What I mean to say is, why would

Mrs. Aquino want Mr. Marcos back in the country where he could disrupt things, make her life harder? Perhaps that's why he wasn't charged."

"No need to apologize," I said. "Just making sure I heard correctly."

"I'm so sorry," he said.

"Now, what if I tell you that during the time of the assassination, Mr. Marcos was seriously ill? He was suffering from lupus. Its complications were actually going to kill him just a few years into his exile."

"I guess he could've still ordered someone else to oversee it, sir. He could've just given the command."

"All right," I said. "You've helped me think this through, Milo. Thank you."

"You're welcome, sir," he said. "So what was the answer?"

"Excuse me?"

"To your first question, sir. What was the right answer? Who killed Ninoy Aquino?"

"Oh, I don't know," I said. "I honestly don't know."

———————

And that was the other possibility I'd thought of as well while driving to Baguio. Perhaps that day Imelda Marcos was going to reveal to Mrs. Aquino the killer's real identity. It is possible that Imelda knew all these years and kept it to herself. After all, when her husband got sick, he gave over much of his responsibility to her. Still, I couldn't think of a good motive on her part for such a revelation, which was why I ruled it out.

You know, Imelda Marcos is also very religious. I heard she

attends mass every Sunday at the Santa Monica Parish Church in Sarrat, Ilocos Norte. In fact, she spent millions of pesos generously restoring that old church when she was still the First Lady. It was where her daughter got married. And there's a monument of Ferdinand standing right outside the town plaza. He is painted in gold.

I've never seen Imelda Marcos in real life. I've watched my share of news reports and documentaries, especially having to do with her Swiss bank accounts. But there's one video, in particular, which stood out to me because it was so different from the rest. In the interview, she was asked about her beliefs. She grabbed a notepad and a pen, and then she drew various shapes to stand in for such abstract concepts as "body," "mind," "soul," or "freedom," using such terms as *the trinity* and *dignity*. I'm sorry, I'm not doing any justice to explaining her beliefs.

Perhaps you could take a look and tell me. *Circles of Life*. I believe that is the title of the book she wrote, not too long ago. I haven't yet had the chance to read it, nor do I think I'll have the chance now. But I think it contains more of her spiritual philosophy, borrowed from such diverse sources as the Kabbalah and binary computing. Her motto, which she's always said she tries to live by, is "Truth, Goodness, and Beauty."

———

You might be surprised to learn that I've thought often of Imelda Marcos and that I have great sympathy for her.

When I was growing up, I constantly saw her on TV, and thought she was not only beautiful and kind but also spoke so eloquently. Throughout my childhood and early teens, she was the one person who was always there, unchanging. I imagine this must be something like how the British view their queen. Imelda, to me and to many others, was like the mother of the country. She was always present in our living rooms.

Once, I watched a biography of her, made by some foreign journalist. It delved into Imelda's own childhood. She was, apparently, very poor—or, to be precise, her family were the poorest relations in a clan of rich families. Her mother had been the second wife, and the children from that first marriage resented their father's new family. Imelda and her siblings had to live in the garage to avoid fighting with those in the main house. She had very little in the way of material things. Her mother died before she was even ten years old.

Imelda sang and strutted her way through college. She worked as a saleslady for a music store in Manila, playing the piano and entertaining customers. She also competed in beauty pageants, and she almost won the Miss Manila contest, you know, coming in as a runner-up. But that wouldn't do for Imelda. She actually went to see the mayor, in tears, to try to change his mind. And here's the crazy part: It actually worked! The mayor overturned the decision and proclaimed Imelda the winner. In the end, of course, all this came out and controversy erupted, so Imelda was instead given the honorary title Muse of Manila.

It would be hard, I think, for anyone not to feel sorry for Imelda. I used to wonder—if only her stepfamily had bucked certain stereotypes and shown her and her mother more compassion, is it possible that history might have been altered? If only she had been blessed with more wealth earlier in life, would she have become as obsessed with it later on? And if she hadn't been so desperate in the beginning, would she still have craved so much power when it came within her reach?

I'm not saying she's not responsible for her own actions. We all are. I'm just saying that because of her upbringing, it seems as though Imelda learned a whole different set of lessons in life. When she became the dictator's wife, it was said she hired a backhoe and razed the garage where she and her family once lived. She banned any books that criticized her or strayed into her less-than-stellar past. She reinvented her story and put herself in portraits, wearing sashes and medals and posing like she was a member of a royal family.

Truth. Goodness. Beauty.

I do think that, in Imelda's mind, she was speaking the truth when she proclaimed that the divine is manifested in our world through beautiful things. "Beauty is love and God made real," I've heard her say. She also often said, without any apparent reservations, that the Filipino people needed to look up to something beautiful amid the ugliness of their poverty. That was why, she said, she took only "a few minutes" to get dressed when she was meeting with her friends, but when she mingled with the commoners, she took hours to prep and preen: "I am both their star and their slave."

I do believe that Imelda meant it in her heart when she said she didn't see her collection of shoes and clothes as extravagant. She is an undiagnosed hoarder. People close to her have said that she's never thrown anything away, that she'd even collect soaps and bottles of lotion from hotel rooms during her travels. "You cannot quantify beauty and love," she said. And that is why she also never considers the prices when she goes shopping.

Imelda herself was almost killed once. At a celebration of her husband's seventh year as president, on December 7, 1972, seventy-seven days after the announcement of martial law, a man wearing a dark suit went up to the stage and stabbed Imelda several times with a bolo knife. "If somebody was going to kill me," she said afterward, "why does it have to be with a bolo? That is so ugly." She said she wished they'd tie a yellow ribbon on the knife to make it look prettier. But she was also convinced that God had spared her because she had been so generous and giving.

That is the truth about Imelda Marcos. I believe she always means every word of what she says. She just sees the world differently, I guess, the way it works, its consequences. She sees herself as set apart by God, who has given her a special character and a special purpose.

And that is why, like many other people who grew up watching her, the mother of our country, I never doubted it when she said to journalists many years ago, "If Ninoy Aquino comes home, he's dead."

We reached Concepcion around one o'clock. It was the hometown of Mr. Aquino, the place where I started working for the family. One block from the octagon-shaped town plaza, there stood the old wooden house with its white arches and dark red shingles.

It always felt strange, going back to this house. Nobody in the family lives there anymore except Manang Dionisia, who was given the task of preserving it. She happened to be in the front yard, pushing her grandson on a training bike, when I honked. I'd forgotten how loud the Crown could be and I gave her quite the fright. She immediately opened the gate to the driveway.

"Do you want me to have a heart attack?" she said, once we'd parked.

"I'm sorry, Manang," I said. "Just checking to see how good your hearing is."

"You could wake up all the dead here with your noise, Lito. Madam, let me help you. I'm sorry, I didn't know you were coming today."

"Thank you," Mrs. Aquino said. "Have you eaten yet?"

"Of course, madam," Manang Dionisia said. "It's well past noon." Manang Dionisia's grandson approached Mrs. Aquino on his bike, took her hand, and placed it on his forehead as a sign of respect. And upon seeing the plastic wrappings of so much fast food, his whole face lit up like a Christmas tree.

———

While Mrs. Aquino went upstairs to take a brief nap, I fixed myself some Sky Flakes and coffee, thinking I'd need the caffeine supplement for the rest of the trip. But that drafty kitchen haunts me to this day. It was where I first met your mother, you know. And her presence—especially the way she used to smile when she saw me, that look of surprise followed by amusement—was still too strong. So I went out to the shed and found some cinder blocks to sit on. Those cinder blocks had been gathered to build the annex that would later become Manang Dionisia's own residence.

"Lito," Manang Dionisia said, with the sound of the screen door shutting behind her. "Just what in the hell is going on?"

"Not much," I said. "Care for a snack?"

"You know what I mean. As good as it is to see you, I'm not sure what you and Madam are doing all the way up here."

I ate another soda cracker. "Well, what did she say?"

"She didn't tell me anything! And of course I couldn't ask her without sounding like I was trying to kick her out of her own house."

"Then perhaps we should leave it at that."

"Okay," she said. "Now I know something is definitely going on."

"It's nothing," I said, which, in hindsight, is always the worst thing you can say, worse even than keeping your mouth shut. But it was too late. I had no choice but to continue my fib. "She just wanted to see the countryside and get some fresh air. We're going back to Manila right after this."

"For the love of God, Lito, she's sick. If something happens to her, you'll be held responsible." She paused. "Does Kris know?"

I shook my head.

"I'll go call her right now."

"No!" I said, spilling some of my coffee.

She gave me the look, that terrible look of a teacher who's caught a student cheating on an exam. And for as long as I breathe, I will never be able to keep a secret from Manang Dionisia. In the next few minutes, I reluctantly told her everything I knew and suspected of Mrs. Aquino's intentions.

Manang Dionisia laughed out loud. "And you think you can get all the way to Baguio in that beat-up car?"

"It's worked so far," I said.

She became serious, even more so than before. She said, "When are you going to start thinking for yourself, Lito." It didn't sound like a question. "Sooner or later, they'll have to know. She *is* their mother."

"Maybe they don't have to," I said.

"Let me put it this way," she said. "I know how much you respect Madam. And that's great. But she's not doing well, and . . ." Manang Dionisia sighed. "Let's just say she won't be around forever, okay? Then what'll happen to you? It's not easy to find a job these days, especially not at our age. Lito, you have to start being more"—and she paused to think about her next word—"flexible. I'm worried for you."

I thanked Manang Dionisia and promised her that I'd seriously consider what she'd said. In turn, she promised she wouldn't tell anyone about our trip. Not yet, at least, not until I had the chance to talk to Mrs. Aquino and sort it all out. I didn't want to break Mrs. Aquino's trust. But until then, I hadn't realized how much of a pickle I'd gotten myself into. Perhaps I *should* think about my future, or what was left of it.

"Did you have a good rest, ma'am?"

We were back on the local road, passing by the wet market, where a crowd had begun to buy vegetables for dinner.

"Very good," she said.

I checked the rearview mirror and saw that Mrs. Aquino did

indeed look better. There was some rosiness to her cheeks. And she had found a paisley scarf with which to wrap her hair, giving her even more color.

"It's funny," she said, "how firm the mattress is upstairs. And to think I used to sleep on it without complaining."

"You made a lot of sacrifices, ma'am, in the past."

"Oh, I wasn't trying to be a martyr. I just didn't realize how bad the bed was back then. If I'd been a princess in that old tale, I'd never have found the pea. You know that story, Lito?"

"Yes, ma'am," I said. "To be honest, I'm not a big fan of it. I never understood what kind of a queen would hide pieces of food to test somebody."

"Well, I think the queen was trying to see if the princess was real."

"And why is that needed, ma'am? Why did a princess have to marry her son? Isn't a good heart enough? Besides, it's a waste of food, if you ask me. And it probably attracted a lot of ants."

Mrs. Aquino laughed. "I think the point might also be about honesty, Lito. Not claiming to be someone you're not."

Clearly our conversation had gotten off on the wrong track. And I had only myself to blame, being so opinionated at the wrong time.

"I guess so, ma'am."

"You know who the queen in the story reminds me of?" she asked.

"Imelda Marcos," I almost blurted, which just shows you how compromised my mind was that day. I said, "No, ma'am."

"My mother-in-law," she said, and it was my turn to chuckle.

"I know what you mean, ma'am. She was, well, shall we say, very particular about things."

"That's putting it mildly. If there was one reason why I tossed and turned in those days, it wouldn't have been the mattress. It would've been wondering if I'd forgotten to unplug all the appliances or made sure all the windows were properly closed. But that's also why the house was kept in such good condition."

"Now that you mention it, ma'am, I remembered something else while I was at the house earlier," I said. "Doña Aurora was the one who interviewed me for the job many years ago."

"That's right," said Mrs. Aquino. "Before we took you to Manila."

"And she did actually put me to a kind of test."

"Really, now?" she said.

"Yes, ma'am."

"Tell me."

"Well, I remember that day there was a plate of fried bananas on the table, which the maid had placed there when our interview started. Sometime in the middle of it, Doña Aurora suddenly stood up and said she had to use the bathroom. She told me that, while waiting for her, I shouldn't be shy to eat the fried bananas on the table. You know I don't refuse food when it's offered to me. As soon as I picked up the fork, I noticed that lying next to the bananas was a mound of loose change. It was just scattered about every which way, such that I don't think anybody would've noticed if a few coins were to go missing. Of course, I wasn't familiar with Doña Aurora back then. Only afterward did I realize how excessively clean she was. She'd never have tolerated such a mess. I imagine that after the interview, ma'am, she counted every last centavo to make sure I hadn't pinched one."

"I've never heard that story," Mrs. Aquino said. "But sounds like it's worked to our advantage, Lito. We ended up hiring an honest man, didn't we?"

"Thanks, ma'am. That means a lot."

"We have Mama to thank for that," Mrs. Aquino said. "I hope she rests in peace."

Looking back, that compliment should've served as the perfect springboard to bring up any topic I desired. I could've asked, very casually, what Mrs. Aquino's kids might make of our trip to see Imelda Marcos. I could have aired my concern about being caught in the middle of things. "Lito," I'd imagine Mrs. Aquino saying. "Just leave it all to me. I'll take care of you."

But I hesitated. For I've never felt comfortable campaigning on my own behalf. That was true then and it still is.

And so the pause that followed, which started as only a fraction of a second, stretched out into a silence. Where it would normally have been awkward not to follow someone's comment with a reply, the delay dragged on, such that puncturing the silence instead became the ultimate act of courage.

I adjusted my seat and allowed my mind to uncoil.

"What should we do with Lito?"

"I told him Mom's been acting funny lately, but he still drove her to Baguio without telling us."

"You can't really fault him. He was probably just following orders."

"That's not an excuse."

"Anyway, she doesn't really need her own driver. What are we keeping him for?"

"Kris, don't say that. He's worked for us as long as you've been alive. He's family."

"Sorry, but I'm just being practical. Maybe we can send him off to work for Pinky."

"Pinky doesn't need another driver."

"Well, if he stays with Mom, it might happen again."

"No, I'll talk to him. I'll make sure he understands."

"We've tried that already."

"Guys, what about the other issue? What do we do?"

"What issue?"

"The thing with Imelda."

"I mean, obviously we need to keep it a secret. Nobody can find out. You're running for office. What if Imelda uses it to her own advantage? What if she uses Mom for good publicity?"

"Maybe you're overthinking this."

"What I know is that it's not right. They've been unrepentant all these years and have denied doing anything wrong. And now we're supposed to be on good terms with them?"

"Lito? Did you hear me?"

"Sorry, ma'am."

"I was saying it's a little warm in here."

"I'll turn up the air conditioner right away, ma'am."

We had just passed the town of Gerona and were approaching Moncada. I estimated we had about two more hours to go before Baguio. The land was flat here—mostly farms and sugarcane fields. There were only a few trees to serve as shelter from the sun's glare.

"Is that better, ma'am?" I hesitated, then turned the air conditioner up one more notch.

"Yes," she said. "Thank you."

But something occurred to me then: I hadn't actually finished refilling the radiator at the gas station that morning. I checked the temperature of the car. The needle was right in the middle of HOT and COLD.

Now, if you own a car, you'll know this doesn't necessarily mean anything. Some cars like a tease, cranking the needle all the way up to the center before graciously staying there. Others, like Mrs. Aquino's SUV, are more predictable, content to stay in the cooler zone. You just have to be very familiar with the particular behavior of your car.

Unfortunately, it had been so long since I'd driven the Crown that I couldn't recall for the life of me how it usually behaved. The warning light hadn't yet turned on. So I decided we'd take our chances, to make up for lost time. I pressed on the gas.

We traveled only for about two more kilometers before the needle peaked. The next thing I saw was smoke rising out of the hood.

7

"THE QUESTION BEFORE us, and for many generations before us, is the question of inequality," Ka Noel said. "Why is it so persistent?"

It was dim inside his hut. The one source of light was Ka Noel, who stood in front of me, holding an antique brass lamp close, as if afraid I'd snatch it and discover what to do with the fire.

I said, "Because some people have more things and others less?"

"But why is that? What happened in the first place?"

"I don't know," I said. "Maybe you're just born into it."

"Or, to be more precise," Ka Noel said, "you're born into a certain kind of family. And we don't get to choose what kind." He picked up a book and, after leafing through its pages, started to read: "The history of all existing society is the history of class struggles..."

This was the start of what Ka Noel called my "education," which I did not ask for and I considered, back then, a serious waste of time. I only followed him because he didn't give me a choice. I answered when he asked me questions, because I didn't want to offend him. But as he droned on, my eyes wandered off to explore the interior of his hut.

A tapestry hung on the wall, covering the window frames. Animals and flowers adorned the patterns; water buffaloes, simplified into outlines, grazed on needles of grass. The thickness of the fabric was what had made the hut so comfortable and fuzzy, I thought, but I wondered if Ka Noel took it down at the height of the dry season. I'd find out, later, that he did not.

"In ancient Rome we have patricians, knights, plebeians, slaves. In the Middle Ages, feudal lords, vassals, guildmasters, journeymen, apprentices, serfs. In almost all of these classes, again, we have subordinate gradations . . ."

Wood carvings of a certain potbellied figure—I think it was a fertility god—were displayed on the shelves along with Ka Noel's books. The largest of these, its chest jutting out, sat close to the floor on top of a black trunk, which looked rather simple in comparison to Ka Noel's other belongings. A silver latch and a big padlock on the trunk glinted as the lamplight moved over them. I quickly returned my gaze to Ka Noel.

"Do you care to read some passages, Lito?" he said. I shook my head. He handed me the book anyway and pointed to a paragraph. He leaned over to share the light, hesitating for a moment before sitting next to me on the couch.

I read aloud, slowly, and with some help from him: "The bourgeoisie . . . wherever it has got the upper hand . . . has put an end to all feudal . . . patriarchal . . . idyllic relations . . . It has pitilessly torn asunder the motley feudal ties"—he corrected my pronunciation of *motley* and I repeated after him—"that bound man to his . . . 'natural superiors' . . . and has left remaining no other nexus . . . between man and man than naked self-interest . . ."

I smelled menthol, and could feel the warm air of his breath. "Should I go on?" I asked, and he nodded.

"It has drowned . . . the most heavenly ecstasies . . . of religious fervor . . . of philistine sentimentalism"—I slowed down on these last words so that he could accompany me—"in the icy water of . . . egotistical calculation."

"Very good," he said. "Now can you finish the rest all by yourself?"

I felt the side of his thigh slightly touching mine before it shifted. I continued to read, "In one word, for exploitation . . . veiled by religious and political illusions . . . it has substituted naked, shameless, direct . . . brutal exploitation."

———

This was to become my new modus with Ka Noel.

Whenever I didn't understand a word, a concept, or a theory, we'd stop, and he'd guide me toward the answer rather than telling me outright. He liked to ask: "What does that word sound like? Does it remind you of anything? If you have to guess, what do you think it means?" He was a very patient man, and gentle, too. He never became upset with me, or anyone, for that matter, as far as I ever saw.

Once, after lending me the Bible and *The Communist Manifesto*, he said, "These two books, Lito, are the only two books you'll ever need in your life. Commit as much of them as you can to memory."

I told him, "I don't believe in memorizing. I heard Einstein never memorized anything he could just look up. A waste of effort, not to mention brain storage."

"Well," he said with a wink, "if you could prove to me that you're using your brain as much as Einstein, I promise I'll leave you alone."

I sat down at my desk one evening with the books Ka Noel had lent me. I grudgingly tried to read and memorize passages, first from *The Communist Manifesto* and then from the Bible, as the former was several folds skinnier, though not much more entertaining, in my opinion.

As I pored over them, I remembered the day my father and I went to the café by the park, when he took me from the boarding school and first told me about Ka Noel. I remembered how my father had clutched the same two books, stopping every now and then as he read to mark some pages with a pen. I wondered what had been so interesting to him. Did he have to endure the same set of questions, and what were his answers? I started to feel a lump in my throat as I wondered about where my father was and how he was doing. I needed to be more like him, I thought, so cool and composed. I picked up the books again and continued reading. When he comes back, I vowed, I'll have a real conversation with him. I'll talk to him about the books we'll read and I will make him proud.

———

I met with Ka Anna often in the mornings, at her garden, or by the creek if there was laundry to do. She'd ask me about the progress of my education, and I was never sure how interested she really was. There were times I even thought she might be mocking me with her replies.

I told her, for example, that I'd found *The Communist Mani-*

festo to be strangely similar to the Old Testament, because there was a lot more anger and spite, more resorting to violence, and a promise for a day of reckoning.

"Oh really?" she said.

Whereas the New Testament, I found, was mostly calmer, more graceful, as if all the rage had already been spent, and God had mellowed quite a bit in his old age.

"Oh really," she said again.

"What do you think?" I finally asked her. We were beating jeans against a bed of rocks.

"About what?" she asked.

"Those ideas," I said. "Or anything else."

"As far as I'm concerned," she said, "there are only two kinds of Communists. Thinkers and doers. The thinkers are the ones who come up with all sorts of theories and grand ideas. The doers, well, they do everything else. They grow the food and they clean the house and they even fight the battles. Except they never get to write any of the books, now, do they? Not even the rules we're supposed to follow. 'Is that fair?' you might ask. Obviously, I'm not a thinker."

"Is that a bad thing?"

"You're the thinker," she said. "You tell me."

"Am I a thinker?" I said.

"Questions, questions, questions. You're beginning to sound like him."

"Ka Noel? Is he a thinker or a doer?"

"Ay!" she said, throwing up her hands. "Look what you've done!" There was a tear—a small one—near the zipper of the pants she was washing. "You're giving me a headache."

I went back to quietly scrubbing my laundry, pouring a

handful of lye, then rinsing it off in the cold current. I took up my bamboo stick and swatted the dirt that remained, repeating the process with the lye.

"Don't get me started with him," Ka Anna said after a while. "That man is whatever he thinks he is."

"I don't actually know him that well," I said.

"Good," she said. "Let's hope it stays that way."

"Why? What do you mean?"

A screeching noise came from a tree on the other side of the creek. Ka Anna turned around and looked up. "Silly bird. Why do you have to be so loud?" she said. "Anyway, we better get on it. I need to head back before lunchtime."

"Can I ask just one more thing?" I said. "Does Ka Noel have, you know, some kind of special powers?"

"That's what they say."

"Have you ever seen it?"

"Me?" she said. "Oh, I try to stay far away from him when he starts doing any funny business. Besides, he's got a lot of fans already. One less person in the crowd doesn't make a difference, does it?" She paused. "Now, between the two of us, there's something you should know."

"What is it?"

She cleared her throat. "Even with all those people around him, admiring him and obeying his every command, I think that, deep down, that man is really a lonely man. And believe me," she said, "a lonely man is the most dangerous kind of man there is."

From Feudalism, we progressed to Colonialism and Imperialism.

I was eating lunch with Ka Noel inside his hut. Lunch was always an unpredictable affair, because Ka Noel depended on the villagers' donations for most of his food. On one hand, the surprise was part of the fun. On the other, it was often the source of agony. That day, Ka Noel opened a can of sardines to add to the boiled squash we received.

"What the friars did was unforgivable," he said. "They parceled out land among themselves, enslaved us, took the women as they pleased." He continued with the theme of tyranny, talking about how the government of Spain, even though it had a proper constitution, was bribed by the priests to look the other way. The friars had so much power, Ka Noel said, that there was one time, after the governor-general who was appointed to the Philippines got into a feud with the archbishop of Manila, when the archbishop and his men stormed the palace and killed the governor in cold blood.

I looked down to see my plate of rice oozing with tomato sauce from the sardines.

"So if you're wondering why you can't speak Spanish, Lito, even if we were colonized for almost four hundred years, it's because the friars didn't want to educate us. For them, our ignorance was their power."

"Oh really," I said.

Ka Noel shifted in his chair. "What's wrong?"

I said nothing. I moved the rice grains around with my fork, piling them into mounds, then crushing those mounds. That was when he touched my wrist.

"I know this must all sound so boring, so remote." He stared at me, his eyes the color of ash, before he softly broke into laughter. "It's incredible. You remind me so much of my younger self." He shook his head. "Just incredible. Lito, we have more things in common than you think."

"Such as?"

"I lost my mother when I was still a child."

I rested the fork on my plate, hid my hands under the table.

"I never knew my father. It was a parish church that took me in. And for a very long time, I was angry. Angry at my parents for abandoning me. Angry at the priest who took care of me. Angry at everyone, angry at the world, really. Then one day the priest said that somebody claiming to be my father had come for me."

Ka Noel took my fork and began to build a rice mound of his own. "He was a coconut farmer. He said he had been searching for me ever since my mother ran away. They'd had a disagreement. He didn't say what it was, only that he was sorry it had taken him a while to find me. But now that he had found me, he asked that I return home with him. Well, that was the biggest choice I had to make in my life. Should I stay with the priest who'd always been kind to me, or go with this total stranger who said he was my father?

"In the end, I chose neither one of them. I went out on my own."

"Were you happy about it?"

"Not at first. But living with myself made me realize I didn't need much to survive. I didn't even need many people around me to be happy. I was often alone, but I was seldom lonely. I became an observer. I observed my surroundings and I learned everything by watching, even before I learned how to read."

He smiled, but then stopped short of sharing the fond memories he seemed to be recalling in his head. Instead, he handed me back my fork. "Finish your food," he said. "And when you're ready, we can go on."

My father came back over that weekend, bringing with him some new books, many of them classics, because his personal funds were running low and that was all he could afford. One of the titles I remember was Jules Verne's *Twenty Thousand Leagues under the Sea*. Another was *Moby-Dick*. I accepted them and put them on the shelf he'd built for me.

But even after a week, I hadn't touched them again.

One day my father said, "Good to know I went out of my way to buy you books so you could turn them into useless knickknacks."

"I'm sorry," I said. "But I just don't like reading them."

"You should've told me earlier."

"Well, you should've told me earlier about the Americans."

"Whatever are you talking about now?"

"Not only did they loot and pillage our land when they occupied us, but did you know that they once shipped off some of our brothers and sisters to St. Louis for an exhibition? The Americans caged them like wild animals. Many of them suffered and died. All this so the Americans could feel better about themselves and pretend they were more civilized."

"That's all in the past."

"Yes, but they've never owned up to it. So until that day comes, I'll never read another book written by an American."

"Is Jules Verne an American?"

"The point is, they're all Westerners. And you can't expect people to just forget about what you did in the past when you've hurt them badly. Like you, disappearing whenever you want to, again and again."

"Are we still talking about the books?"

"You're so slow," I said.

"You're a disrespectful son," he said.

Then, before I could stop myself, I shot back, "You're the worst father."

He slapped me.

Today, this particular incident takes up barely any space in my mind. But such exchanges add up, and contribute to why we inevitably become distant from our family and loved ones. In the course of a lifetime, each moment may seem rather trivial and silly. But once a phrase is uttered or an action carried out, we can never take it back.

I apologized to him before the night was over. And he responded in kind. He said he'd been under a great deal of stress lately. I tried to ask why but he said he preferred not to tell me, that it was for my own good. He wasn't sure if what he'd been doing down in Moncada would eventually get him into trouble. It was for the cause, though, he kept saying, which he believed in with his whole heart. Someday, he said, when the nation had progressed and become more equal, people would thank him for all he'd done.

———

"Perhaps it is my fault," Ka Noel said, "for making it sound like I'm all for a black-and-white way of thinking. Truth is, I'm for using everything that you can get your hands on, as long as it makes sense."

"So I can read books in English?" I asked.

"Think of it this way. What is the single most important thing that the colonizers and oppressors took away from us?"

"Our wealth?"

"You've turned far more Marxist than I thought." He laughed. "Aside from that."

"Freedom?" I said.

"Exactly. Now, which do you think gives you more freedom and power: Being able to read only certain books? Or the ability to read any books in any language you want?"

That paradox—that one could consciously use the colonizer's language as a tool for building one's own freedom—is the singular lesson from Ka Noel that has stayed with me to this day, since I've consciously unlearned the rest of his teachings.

"Here," he said. "Let's take a break from history." He handed me a pair of books by two new, unlikely authors—Gerard Manley Hopkins and Henry David Thoreau. "What do you make of that? A Jesuit and an American."

———

It occurred one afternoon before my father was to go back to the lowlands.

I was foraging by myself in the woods, reciting my poems as I went. I had discovered, through Ka Anna, that nobody likes to listen to someone who breaks out in poetry in the middle of a conversation. I used to be able to do that, you know. I could pull out lines from Hopkins, and I reveled in the great serenity of nature. I'd project my voice onto the trees, my captive audience:

"The world is charged with the grandeur of God. It will flame out, like shining from shook foil . . ."

Anyway, I'm too old to remember much of that now. Just bits and pieces, here and there. But that day, I wasn't alone. I heard a voice call out:

"It gathers to greatness, like the ooze of oil crushed."

Ka Noel emerged from the bushes, holding a blunt spear. I said, "You shouldn't sneak up on a person like that!"

He laughed. "There's no need to be afraid here. The forest is a sanctuary. Only when you leave it for the world of man should you be afraid."

"I wasn't afraid. I only meant it was cruel."

"Then I'm sorry," he said. "I didn't mean any harm."

We walked together for a few minutes, he asking me about my progress through his books, and I telling him that I wished to have my own Walden Pond someday. "I'm beginning to realize the difference between loneliness and solitude," I said. "One is involuntary, while the other—"

"Shhhh." He put a finger to his lips. "Did you hear that?" I said I didn't, before he shushed me again.

He went down on his knees, his spear at the ready. And, just like a spider on the hunt, he jumped into some thick bushes. I waited for him to emerge. But all was quiet.

"Ka Noel?" I said. "Where are you?"

There was no response. Deciding not to let my imagination get the better of me, I told myself he must've just pursued his quarry farther into the woods. I picked up my basket and left.

When I reached our hut, my father was seated, reading the

newspaper with his legs crossed. I suspected it was several days old, as we did not get any deliveries up in the mountains.

"There have been riots near the palace," he said. "Marcos is threatening to force martial law."

For a moment it felt strange to be hearing about such events. We were so cocooned in the village it was easy to forget about the rest of the world. Nor did I care about what my father was saying. I was curious about something else altogether.

"Where did you get the paper?" I asked.

"This isn't good," he said. "Once that happens he'll be able to arrest anybody. Ka Noel said we needed to be more careful from now on."

I repeated my question.

"From him, of course," my father said. "He was here for coffee." I looked at the table and saw two dirty mugs.

"And were you with him the whole time I was out?" I asked.

"The whole afternoon," he said. "Why?"

"Nothing," I said. "Just wondering."

I did not tell my father about my encounter with Ka Noel in the forest. I knew it was quite impossible for a man to be in two places at one time, or to travel that fast. I also didn't tell my father, because it dawned on me, as I thought back to the moment in the forest, that I'd met Ka Noel near the outgrowth of a large ficus tree.

———

I'm not sure when we first started to take naps, but it must've been well into the dry season, because by that point the heat would have been intense outside, and unbearable inside Ka

Noel's hut if not for his battery-powered fan. I think I must've slept on the couch, and because the fan didn't swivel, I think Ka Noel must have given me exclusive use of it. Such a kind gesture would have been very much in his character. Anyway, I can't really remember. All I know is that it wasn't long before I started taking my rest next to him on his bed.

A funny thing is that he reminded me of my old roommate, at the boarding school. The minute he touched a flat surface, he fell asleep. He snored, too. It sounded like the bellowing of a cow, with the occasional snort and grunt. I could never sleep during those nap periods. And I didn't want to ask for something to plug my ears, because I didn't want him to think I was soft.

Once, I played a dirty trick on him, Ka Noel.

See, I'd learned from the boys in school that it's when someone is deeply asleep that one has the best chance to ask him questions and get an honest reply. Our senses are wired, I think, to be half-aware of the things going on in our surroundings, even while sleeping, in case a predator comes pounding in. But we're not so aware as to put up mental defenses. After all, few lions or wolves would stop to interview a sleeping human before devouring him.

So I waited until I heard that terrible noise coming from Ka Noel's throat. Then I said softly, "Tell me the truth now. Do you really have superpowers?"

He grunted.

I didn't know what to make of that answer, if it even was one, so I asked again. "Do you or do you not have superpowers? Simple yes or no."

"Yes," he mumbled.

I was shocked that the trick had actually worked! I wanted to laugh, and then I wanted to call a witness to stand beside me and confirm what I'd just heard. But I calmed myself down. I had a few more questions in mind.

"Tell me, what is inside the black trunk?"

He snorted.

Oh, it had to be yes-or-no, I thought. It took me a full minute to ask again.

"Is what's inside the trunk something I should be afraid of?"

"Yes," he said, clearer this time.

"Is it something magical?"

"Yes."

"Does anyone else in the village know about it?"

"Yes," he said.

"Who?"

I was about to reframe the question when I heard him say, "Anna. Her husband."

To be honest, I wasn't actually sure about those three words, because Ka Noel grunted and turned to his other side, hitting my elbow in the process. He woke up.

"What are you doing?" he asked, as if his very life were in danger. I smiled like a dog.

———

The next time I was at the creek with Ka Anna, I noticed she was washing some fatigues and undershirts. I seized the opportunity to ask if they were her husband's.

"You know," I said, "it's a little strange to me how we've already spent so much time together but I've not heard much about him."

"What's there to talk about?" she said. "He's just like any man. They eat a lot. Sleep and drink a lot. Fart a lot."

I laughed. But I was undeterred by her strategy. In my experience, when someone jokes out of the blue like that, it's often to hide a secret. It's the people hurting inside who tend to crack the most jokes.

"Can I meet him sometime?"

"I already told you," she said. "He's always out in the jungle, training. If not, he's being sent on a mission somewhere else."

"Okay," I said. "It's just that he's like a mystery."

"You never talk about your father, either," she said. "What does that mean?"

"But I do."

"Do you?" But then, perhaps as a friendly gesture to ward off my pestering, she said, "He might come by this Sunday, for mass."

"You know anything about a black trunk?" I was hoping that the abrupt switch would catch her off guard. I watched her for any signs of recognition, but none came.

"What's with all the silly questions today?" she said. "Go back to work."

If she thought she'd escaped my prying forever, Ka Anna had seriously miscalculated. For I hadn't forgotten. And if there was someone more dangerous than a lonely man, it was probably a man with nothing better to do.

The days withered away like the plants in my parched garden. I continued my education with Ka Noel, but I was getting rather tired of it. He must have sensed this, because he, too, would find things to discuss other than doctrine and theology and poetry. He told me many more stories. And as the heat worsened, our naps got longer and longer.

Once, while he was asleep, I snuck from the bed and lit a low flame over the lamp. I tiptoed to the window frame and found the black trunk resting underneath. The latch and the padlock had become all too familiar—they were the things my eyes focused on whenever my mind drifted during Ka Noel's lectures. I studied the trunk for any other cracks or openings. If I could only move the metal lid with some kind of lever, I thought, I might be able to take a peek inside. I tried lifting the trunk a little to test its weight. I could hear a lot of small things rolling inside. It seemed light enough that I could easily pull it about half an inch off the floor. But I wasn't careful enough, and the lamp had been set too dim, because I didn't see the potbellied figure losing its balance when I lowered the trunk. The wooden deity toppled over and crashed to the floor.

Ka Noel woke up and saw that I had chipped his statue. He clutched it to him like a dead pet and told me that we were finished with our lessons. I asked if he meant it just for that day, or for good. He said, "I don't know yet." He didn't look angry, just very sad and disappointed.

I didn't see him again until that Sunday. He performed all the rituals as expected in his fine vestments, and a part of me felt proud of the fact that I knew the man on the pulpit better than most of the villagers there. I could even begin to appreciate the strangeness of the Eucharist. These rituals weren't just symbolic, I realized; they allowed people to share in acts that became predictable over time, a form of stability that is welcomed, and looked forward to, when your existence lies outside of society and is threatened every day.

That thought led me back to Ka Anna and her husband. I searched for her and found her in the back row, alone. I could tell that she had painstakingly ironed her dress—not an easy thing to do, by the way, using hot coals.

After the benediction, I made a beeline for the rations table, where Ka Anna had started handing out baskets. I asked her where he was, and she pretended not to know who I meant. Her husband, I reminded her.

"Oh right," she said. "He's sleeping."

"On a Sunday?"

"What's wrong with that?"

"But you said—"

"And where is *your* father?" She was suggesting a kind of false equivalency.

"He's arriving," I said. "Later. And I'm not lying."

"I'm glad," she said. "Say hi to him for me."

"I will," I said. "Goodbye."

If you've been paying attention, you can probably guess what I did next. After I left the basketball court, I ran and ran until I reached Ka Anna's hut. But it was locked, as you might have suspected, and nobody answered. So I climbed a trellis, in through her window, and found myself in the bedroom. Never before had I been inside her house, other than in the living room. It was spotless, the bed properly made, the sheets folded and neatly tucked, and not a soul was present. Not on the bed or on the couch or anywhere else. As I entered the last corner of the hut— her kitchen—it was the smell that greeted me first, that sour stench of fermentation.

Lined up on her shelves were bottles upon bottles of pickled vegetables—the ladyfingers, eggplants, peppers, cabbages, all the familiar friends from the garden I'd helped her grow, and even some bright red berries—bubbling and rotting away slowly, uneaten and untouched.

If this was a play, at this point the rest of the stage would go dim except for the spotlight on our protagonist. Time would stop temporarily so the character could talk to himself. It is a common technique, and the character's monologue is given a rather pretty-sounding name: "soliloquizing." In real life, however, we usually call this kind of thing "going crazy."

After I saw Ka Anna's cupboard, I asked myself a series of questions out loud, then answered them myself.

"Why did Ka Anna lie about her husband?"

"She lied to you because he's either nonexistent or dead."

"Did she do it on purpose, or is she imagining things?"

"It could be both."

"Is this connected to the injury Ka Noel talked about?"

"Maybe. And it's possible she might even have killed her husband."

"That's far-fetched."

"Why? It could've been an accident. Or he could've lost his life to save her. Why all this secrecy if it doesn't stem from guilt?"

"I guess."

"It's possible she might have killed your mother, too."

"Now you're crossing the line."

"It might've happened around the same time."

"Stop it."

"Why would you care? You don't know your own mother."

"I said stop it."

"Okay. Shall we talk about Ka Noel, instead? Tell me all the things you want to do to him."

"He's like a second father."

"Lito, you don't have to lie to me, too."

And that was when, I remember, I was seized with an impulse that started out as a small round image, like I was watching through a pinhole camera, with Ka Noel napping on the bed in the dark, and me toying with the tiny flicker of the lamp, raising it higher and higher so I could admire the beauty of the tapestry hanging on the wall, the intricate designs of the flowers and the beasts of burden—and then I watched them as they were first singed by the flame, which licked them at the edges slowly and deliberately, until it roared into an all-consuming blaze.

"Stop it," I said.

But I couldn't. The more I resisted the idea, the more eagerly my mind tried out different ways to do it. I was filled with rage. I wanted Ka Noel to burn along with his hut.

"Question: Are you a solitary man, Lito, or a lonely one?"

8

I LAY AWAKE the whole of last night, just thinking.

At some point I drifted off and dreamed I was talking to someone about things I have no business telling anyone, things I've always kept to myself and which, frankly, I don't think are all that interesting. Of course, it wasn't a dream but a memory— a recent memory.

You really are losing it, Lito.

This morning I resumed my reading of Ferdinand Marcos. I was at the part where he wrote about creating the "New Society." He bragged that the Philippines would serve as a model for the entire world for how to achieve quick and radical reforms. I sighed. What really happened of course was that Mr. Marcos and his friends got richer during this time while the rest of the economy started to tank.

Then the nurse came in. It was a girl this time. She had tied her hair in a pretty blue ribbon dotted with stars. She was about Milo's age, I guessed, but unlike him, she was very svelte. She moved about with grace. I had the thought that she wouldn't last in this country—she'd go abroad the first chance she got, as our best and brightest do, unfortunately.

As she was swabbing the crease on my elbow, I asked her about Milo. She said he had been taken sick. I said I hoped he didn't catch anything from me. She said, "I'm sure it's just minor. I checked on him before I left home."

"Oh, I see. And you must be his . . . ?"

"Housemate," she said. "We went to nursing school together."

"Is that right?"

"Yes. I admit, at some point we were sort of a thing. But that was a long time ago. We're just friends now. Good friends."

I have to say I was rather impressed at how quickly she revealed herself to me, relating things most people might consider rather private. Also, she said all this without any sign of nerves. I could feel the steadiness in her hand as she stuck the needle right into me.

"Does he ever talk about the old man, the one with the heart and kidney condition, who complains too much?" I asked cheekily.

"Not at all," she said.

"I guess I'm not that memorable."

"Don't be silly," she said. "You know we follow strict confidentiality rules."

"I was just kidding," I said.

She nodded and patted my arm lightly.

"The thing about Milo," she offered, "is that he often appears clueless, or likes to pretend that he is, so that people leave him alone. When we used to date, I had to work to pull out how he truly felt about things—like what movie he wanted to watch, or which restaurant to go to. Otherwise, he'd keep saying, 'I don't mind if you decide for me.'"

"Maybe he really doesn't mind."

"Oh, if only you really knew him!"

She gave me a piece of gauze and told me to apply pressure on the spot from which she'd just taken out the needle.

"Mind if I ask what you do?" she said.

I told her the facts, then added, "Former driver. In better times."

"*The* Mrs. Aquino?"

"How many of her could there be?"

She looked at me, then at the glass vial in her hand, as if deciding whether I was telling the truth based on the viscosity of my blood.

Finally, she said, "So what was she like?"

Ah, that perennial question—the answer to which depends not so much on me but on the person asking and what I take to be their motives. If they seem to want a good gossip, then I just tell them a few dry details. If they seem earnest enough to want to know the truth, well, then I carefully choose something worth telling. But Mrs. Aquino's gone now, I thought, so maybe I can relax a little.

That is a luxury of old age, I guess—one can care less.

People always say that Ferdinand Marcos was the most cunning and intelligent president we've ever had. I've heard this over and over, not just from his supporters, but even from a few journalists whose objectivity I trust. Nowadays, especially, they say, "If only Mr. Marcos wasn't kicked out so suddenly, if only he'd had more time, the Philippines would be as great as Singapore today!" They always like to bring up the case of Singapore, precisely because they equate a strongman with a savior. But Mr. Marcos was in power for twenty-one years! If that isn't enough time for one person to fix things, I don't know what is.

Mrs. Aquino, on the other hand, served only a few years. It was she who voluntarily stepped down and imposed a term limit on herself. She decided things by consensus, you know, which does tend to slow down some actions, I admit. But that's not necessarily a bad thing. Mrs. Aquino was cunning in a way people never gave her credit for. She was just not one to boast.

"What was she like?" I asked the nurse. "She was someone who preferred to be quiet but who could surprise you. Someone you could deeply miss."

———

They say that truth is stranger than fiction. And if what I've been telling you wasn't a true story, you'd be right to be suspicious about the series of coincidences that happened after the Crown overheated.

Mrs. Aquino and I had found ourselves stuck on the very outskirts of my hometown. Since it was a holiday, there was not much local traffic. All the cars were just passing through on their way to somewhere much farther off. The few drivers who stopped to check on us were sorry when I told them we had engine problems. They said we'd need a tow to the nearest town. The repair was something that would require a lot of time and effort, as I'd known all along.

After my last attempt at convincing a friendly car to help us, Mrs. Aquino came out of hiding in the backseat. "I'll steer," she said. "You push."

"All the way, ma'am?"

"Well, we can't just sit here and wait. You have other ideas?"

"All right, ma'am."

I replaced the prop rod and secured the hood. I walked slowly to the back of the car, hoping to discover a new solution on the way, or for Mrs. Aquino to change her mind. But she just closed the door to the driver's seat.

Part of me felt like I deserved this punishment. I should've known better than to take risks with the Crown earlier, not in this heat, when the air conditioner was running at its fullest. But there was also that persistent voice telling me that I'd been fully aware of what I was doing. I had wanted an escape from my moral dilemma, and I saw an opportunity to abort the mission. Perhaps Mrs. Aquino had guessed this as well.

"Ma'am, I'm ready whenever you are," I said. "Don't forget to release the hand brake."

She waved at me to go ahead.

So I pushed and she steered. I pushed and pushed some more until I thought we'd made good headway. But the Crown had moved forward only a few meters in total. I had trouble breathing and my chest felt very tight.

"Did you release the hand brake?" I shouted in between gasps. I gave it a rest.

Mrs. Aquino stepped out of the car. "Are you okay?" she asked. I nodded, still panting.

"You sure?" she said. "Do you want some water?" I shook my head.

Then she stated the obvious: "Lito, I don't think this is going to work after all."

"Watch out!" I said.

A cargo truck zoomed past us, blaring its horn.

"Ma'am," I said. "Maybe it's time we call for help. Ask one of your kids to come pick us up. Meantime, we can take a bus to Concepcion and wait at the old house with Manang Dionisia."

Mrs. Aquino didn't look pleased. She kept fussing with her fingernails. "So that's it, then, huh?" she said. "We came all the way here for nothing."

"I'm sorry, ma'am."

"It's okay," she said. "It's not your fault."

Mrs. Aquino went to get her purse from the backseat. I was still holding on to the trunk for balance because I felt a bit dizzy. I didn't know then that something was wrong with my heart. Years later, it would cause me the same type of pain, but several times worse. Back then I thought I only needed more exercise, which I eventually tried, and to go on a diet, which I never did.

When she reappeared, Mrs. Aquino had her cell phone cradled in the crook of her neck. Soon one of her kids would come pick us up, I thought, and our troubles would be over.

And then she raised her hand. She wasn't looking at me, though, but at something far away. She started waving, hesitantly at first, then vigorously, with both hands. I turned to see what all the fuss was about. I sighed, and then I laughed. It was an oxcart laden with sugarcane, drawn by two buffaloes.

———

I'm sure we were quite a sight to behold: the farmer, gripping the harness, flanked by a bald, round fellow and an elegant lady in a paisley scarf. Behind us we dragged the old overheated car, hooked to a hemp rope tied in a complicated chain of knots. And atop the car rested the nest of sugarcane stalks. We paraded into town in search of a repair shop.

Little had changed in Moncada, as far as I could tell. There were new stores here and there, signs, some might think, of commercial progress. But the overall scenery was still that of a dusty rural town dominated by sugarcane fields. I'm not talking down on it, don't get me wrong. In fact, this town, as well as several like it nearby, is the kind of quintessential Filipino town that politicians would like us to imagine whenever we talk about our heritage. Oh, those hardworking farmers with hearts of gold, carrying their hoes or pulling their plows, tasked not just with providing the people with vegetables and fruits, but also with nationalistic pride in a country always yearning for more.

You know, the strange thing about going back to the place of one's childhood is not that people change—that's quite natural— but that you expect them somehow to stay the same in the way they treat you. In other words, you expect them to still think of you, where you used to live and walk, the people you interacted with, your habits and your rituals, as if you were still with them. But the ghost you left behind is really the last thing people want to think about. A place may change little, yes, but it changes a great deal in terms of how it remembers you. And so you are surprised every time you realize the ways in which you've been forgotten.

We couldn't find an open repair shop. But we chanced upon a vulcanizing shack, the proprietor of which happened to have a brother who owned an auto supply store. When the proprietor saw Mrs. Aquino, he said he was going to call his brother to come fix our car immediately.

"Good God," he said. "If I knew such people as yourself were coming my way, ma'am, I'd have prepared some bread and juice. I'm sorry, I have nothing to offer right now. Would you care for some boiled eggs? Or coffee, perhaps? Pakshit, you do look exactly like her on TV. I meant, of course, you are her. Jesus. Pardon my language, ma'am. Have I been cursing at you all this time? Pakshit."

"No need to apologize," Mrs. Aquino said. "I'm just very thankful for your help."

"There, I've forgotten my manners again," he said. "Would you please have a seat, ma'am? And you, too, sir? Those benches are not the most comfy, I'm afraid. But my brother should be here soon. He lives just around the corner."

I took the side closest to the road, in case I needed to protect Mrs. Aquino. Nobody else was in the shack, but it was small enough that the three of us made a crowd. Outside sat a big rubber cauldron filled with dirty water, the kind in which tire tubes would be submerged to locate a leak. When we were kids, sometimes we inflated those tubes out at the beach and used them as rafts. Nowadays, most cars have the tubeless tires, but that shows you the prevailing fashion in this town.

"By the way, ma'am," the proprietor said, "I'm so sorry to hear about your condition. I saw the news. My sister had that same type of cancer. Very nasty. Killed her in just a few weeks after being diagnosed."

"I'm sure everyone's case is different," I said.

"Of course," the proprietor said. "I don't mean to say— Pakshit."

"Please accept my condolences," Mrs. Aquino said.

We were saved by the man's brother, who came just in time to defuse the awkwardness. They had very similar features and wore their moppy hair with a trim mustache, except the brother wore eyeglasses, which made him seem more serious, if not downright meek.

I asked Mrs. Aquino if I could leave her for a while. She gave me a look I could not quite understand. It could have meant either "Don't leave me here," or "Why are you even asking me?" But then she nodded.

It turned out that the radiator hose of the Crown had burst. That was the bad news, because the replacement would take at least an hour. The good news, on the other hand, was that the engine had been spared. I asked the brother if his store happened to carry the needed parts for an older car. "Of course," he said. "If I had a choice, I'd only work with cars like yours. They don't make them like they used to."

"That's true," I said.

"You know, you look very familiar," he said. "Any chance we know each other from somewhere?"

I said I wasn't sure.

"You're not from around here, are you?"

"No, no," I said. "I'm from Zambales. You must have the wrong person."

"Maybe," he said. "But you sure look very familiar." He gave me a big smile and I noticed that some of his molars were missing.

When we got back to the shop, Mrs. Aquino was holding a half-eaten egg and seemed to be choking. I almost rushed to her rescue before I realized she was just laughing away with the proprietor, as if the two of them were old friends.

There was a church across the road that Mrs. Aquino said she wanted to visit. And so it was arranged that we would wait there until the Crown was fixed. While crossing the street, I noticed a very curious thing—I seemed to recognize the plate numbers of some of the cars that passed us. Was I imagining things, or could it be that these were the very same cars that used to pick my classmates up and drop them off at school?

A long time ago, I used to just sit by the stairwell on the ground floor of our school and watch people come and go. While other kids were playing marbles or hide-and-seek, I far preferred solitude and the art of sitting. Over the course of a few months, and not particularly out of any ambition on my part—more like osmosis, I guess—I began to memorize the plate numbers of the cars that passed by me. There's a poetry in them, believe me, as certain combinations of letters and numbers are more memorable than others. "LBC 213" has those nice long vowels, whereas "TKX 655" is wonderfully choppy. I think what makes these patterns poetic is that they're forced into a kind of form—three letters followed by three numbers. Sometimes the staccato resembles a marching command, immediately demanding attention from its observer: "RFU 349"!

Anyway, I wouldn't be surprised if the cars no longer belonged to the same people. They might have been sold to others in town. It didn't matter. But the idea that those plate numbers somehow lived on, that maybe some boy or girl was reciting them like I used to and finding poetry in them—this odd idea warmed my heart considerably.

I followed Mrs. Aquino as she picked up a candle and walked from one chapel to another. It felt like a mistake, what I was doing. But I didn't want to just leave her by herself. So I trailed her by a few steps, until we reached the transept and she placed the candle outside the gate of Our Lady of Fatima. We then took our seats in the back pew, where she knelt down to pray.

Even though I've never been religious, I've always cherished the serenity afforded by churches, the way space is constructed so one has freedom of movement and one's eyes are drawn upward by the tall pillars. At that moment, I wasn't thinking so much of God. Rather, I was thinking that for most people in this country, our local parishes boasted the finest interiors we'd ever see in our lives. Malls and city halls may be big, but they're functional, for the most part. Churches, however, are meant to inspire awe.

While we were inside, a boy approached the pulpit, accompanied by a guitarist. I imagine they'd chosen to practice at a time when the church was rather empty. The lyrics, which I didn't recognize, were in Tagalog and were filled with a sense of longing. He was young enough that his voice could still hit all the high notes, echoing briefly against the wooden ceiling before dissipating. I shivered every time, perhaps because I was rooting for him, and didn't want to share in his shame if he missed any notes. And I remember vividly that he reminded me of you.

I know it sounds strange, if not a little silly, because that was almost ten years ago now, when you'd have been in your mid-thirties. But I often still think of you as a naughty six-year-old, since that's what you were the last time I saw you in person. You were always a little sweaty, your mother always chasing you down for a bath.

———————

Did I ever tell you that your mother has sent me only three pictures of you in your whole life? I suppose you might not even know that she sent me any pictures at all. But it was my only way of connecting with you. I hope you don't mind.

There was that high school portrait, your smile still adorable amid the braces, the pair of dimples perfectly intact. Then there was an official picture with an embossed seal from a college in San Francisco, where she said you'd studied political science, and graduated with honors. Afterward, you moved to the capital to work for a newspaper, where you married another journalist. The two of you looked so happy together in that wedding photo. You were still in your twenties then, and wearing a tux. But I thought you'd grown to be such a mature and good-looking man.

It was only years later that I found out from your mother that you'd gone back to live with her in California. I think she must've felt guilty about sharing all those images without your permission, because she stopped talking to me for a time. But I did my best to pry.

Eventually I learned that you had gotten a divorce, and that you'd lost your job when your newspaper company closed down. She admitted that you'd been depressed and that she felt very helpless about it. I hope you don't mind me knowing this. Your mother told me only because I insisted she do so, so the fault lies entirely with me.

In any case, I wish I could've done something about your troubles. I would've flown there to see you in a heartbeat, if I could. But, you know, someone like me would be denied entry right away, because they'd suspect that I would overstay my visa, which I might very well do, since I'd have nothing to lose. I even entertained the idea that perhaps it might do *you* good to take a break and come stay with me. I don't believe you've ever been back here, to the Philippines, and I always wondered how you'd see it as an adult. What would you think of this place today, and what could we have offered you that you don't already have over there?

But, no, I was quite sure that there were many other countries that you'd consider visiting first. I hear the beaches in Thailand are pristine. The food in Indonesia and Malaysia is colorful and diverse. And the culture and history in Japan or Korea or Taiwan are richer and painstakingly preserved. Even when I think of our best churches—the Manila Cathedral, the San Agustin Church, the Paoay Church, to name a few—none of them can rival the ones in Europe, from which we've derived our imitations. So we have nothing much here, I'm afraid. And I say this with great sadness, because I wonder where we went wrong. I think that all these countries were poor at one time, but they've managed to overcome their poverty. Is there something in us, then, we Filipinos, that makes our characters gravely flawed?

Sitting in that church, staring at the stained-glass windows depicting the Stations of the Cross, I thought that even religion had failed to save us. Did it make us more honest than our neighbors? Did we commit fewer crimes and become less corrupt because of our love of Jesus? Or perhaps we've been so poor for so long that we can no longer afford to be virtuous? For what is honesty or virtue, when you're watching your son or daughter or father or mother waste away and starve?

I've said before that I think the land has an amazing capacity for memory. What I mean to say is that people come and go—we are born and then we die—but the land remains. The land has witnessed all the injuries we've suffered. Far more so than its people, it would be in the best position to answer the question of whatever happened to the Philippines. Because the Aquinos always blamed the Marcoses; the Marcoses blamed the Communists and the Muslims; the Communists and the Muslims blamed American imperialism; the Americans blamed the Japanese and fascism; the Japanese blamed Western colonialism; the colonialists blamed the uncivilized natives; and so on till the dawn of time.

Does this mean that nobody is to blame, or everybody is?

I don't know. It's no surprise, perhaps, that most of us have given up already. Ours is a history of sorrow without clear redemption in sight. Which is probably also why, I thought as I sat there in the church, listening to the boy, so many of us love to sing, and sing so well. Scientists would probably explain our innate talent in terms of genes—perhaps the vocal cords of the Filipinos are somehow longer or thicker. But I'd like to think otherwise. I think we sing so well because singing has become our armor, the way our bodies have responded to centuries of brutality, our longing to be free.

And when I come to think further about the earlier question of what we have to offer the world, I realize that I was a bit hasty. In the first place, we don't in fact owe anyone a favor, nor are we obligated to offer up anything of ours. We may not have the landmarks that the average tourist seeks, but we do have a resilient people. And for better or for worse, and rather incredibly, we have chosen not to hold on to any grudge or anger. We've chosen to forgive, and to forgive rather easily. This is the amazing quality that makes us so warm and openhearted, but also allows us to be abused, to be tricked, to be hurt, over and over again.

As I sat there looking at Mrs. Aquino with her head bowed and her eyes closed, I felt my blood pressure begin to rise and my palms to sweat. "Ma'am," I finally said. "With all due respect, what makes you think you have the right to forgive Imelda Marcos?"

———

And Mrs. Aquino rose up from her prayer, looked at me, and said, "I've been asking myself the same thing."

She took off her eyeglasses and began wiping them with her scarf. "Lito," she said, "do you believe in ghosts?"

I said that I did not.

She nodded. "This afternoon when I was taking a nap back in the old house, I thought I might've seen my husband. Actually, I did see him, and I got to talk to him. I said, 'If you're who you claim to be, then swear upon your mother's grave that you are real.' And he did just that. I thought to myself, If I am just imagining things, would I ever be so brazen as to make someone swear a falsehood upon my mother-in-law? No, I'm too terrified of that woman. So I concluded right there and then that Ninoy was actually present. Am I crazy to say that?"

I said nothing.

She continued: "The first thing I noticed was that he was wearing the same shirt as on the day he boarded the plane.

Cream-colored, with extra-long lapels, very stylish back then. Except his clothes were clean. I told him, 'Don't tell me you've disobeyed your mother and gone ahead and washed your shirt?' Because, of course, his mother ordered everyone not to touch the body after he was shot. She wanted the clothes to be saved, no matter how bloodied they were. 'I'm fine,' he said. 'And she's fine, too, by the way. I have merienda with her from time to time. So, you know, swearing by her grave doesn't mean much these days, with it being empty and all.'

"I didn't find it funny and I told him not to laugh at me. I said he was being mean. And then, I don't know why, I couldn't control myself, I began to cry. 'Don't cry,' he said. 'I was just joking.' And I said, 'How could you?' He asked why I was so cross with him over a little joke. And I said, 'How could you have done it to us, knowing all along you were going to get yourself killed?' He said, 'Are you really still thinking about that, after all these years?' He looked like he wanted to defend himself, which he was always good at.

"But I wasn't done yet and I didn't give him the chance. I said, 'You know, that night, the kids saw the news on TV. I had to try to put them to bed, afterward. Imagine, how could I explain to them that you had gone away for good? So I improvised, saying something about your principles, your hope that things would change for the better back home. I said you thought returning to the Philippines was the right thing for you to do, and that was very important. And, you know, they actually believed me! I was surprised that they did. I was afraid one of them—especially Ballsy—would ask, "But why did he decide to go back? What kind of a father would abandon his own children?" And maybe that was just me putting words into their mouths. Because what I really wanted to ask was "What kind of a husband?"'

"'Come on, dear,' he said. 'You're making it sound like the whole thing was my fault. Remember, I was the one who took the bullet. Right here at the back of my head. See? Did I know what would happen to me? Yes, it was always a possibility, but I wanted to think I had a chance, that our enemies wouldn't be so callous or stupid. I had to believe it.'

"'Would you still have done it today,' I asked, 'knowing what we know now to be true?'

"He gave this some thought and said, 'I'm afraid I would.'"

Mrs. Aquino folded her glasses, only to open and close them again, as if she were testing the strength of the hinges.

"He said, 'Dear, I'm sorry if that's a hurtful thing to say, but I'm just being honest. I can't isolate my actions based on the end result. That's the way to perdition. Think about it. Wasn't there ever a time when you had to make a decision, but you knew that the outcome would leave everyone unhappy?'

"I told him I didn't know. And that I was just tired. I said that I missed him—I always have. People often said that it would get better with time, but I told him I thought it was becoming worse for me, because look at me, now I'm all alone. I wish that he could just come back, even if just to spend a few hours with me. We could sit outside and stare at the clouds, for all I care. 'Don't worry,' he said. 'It won't be much longer until we meet again.' Then he disappeared."

Mrs. Aquino put her glasses back on. She sighed. "I might have just been hallucinating, Lito. I've been warned this may be a side effect of my treatment."

I nodded. I was trying to imagine what her husband might have looked like in her dream. I could only think of him when he was young and healthy, as he was when I briefly worked for him.

"You know," Mrs. Aquino said, "when we were at that car shop earlier, and I was talking to the owner, I kept wondering if I could've done more to help him. When I was still in office, I mean. People always talk about legacy, but to tell you the truth, most days back then were a blur. You were shuttled from one meeting to another and you were lucky if you could catch something decent to eat. Perhaps that's where I failed, Lito. I was so overwhelmed that I ended up not doing enough to make an impact. And here I am now, on my way to Baguio. Isn't it selfish of me to pursue my own little peace when so many people are still suffering?"

The young boy was still singing and the guitar still being played in the background. So I didn't hear the footsteps until the man was right behind me, tapping me on my shoulder. It was the proprietor's brother. He told us that the Crown was ready.

9

I'VE THOUGHT ABOUT that moment many times. If we'd waited inside the church awhile longer, how would I have responded to Mrs. Aquino? There was a frighteningly good deal she didn't know about me. She didn't know, for example, that the town we were stuck in was my hometown. I'd never found a reason to tell her. She also didn't know that I'd once lived in the mountains of Zambales with a group of people that many today would call a cult. And though I once told her my father was a businessman, Mrs. Aquino knew little else about him. I guess I should consider myself lucky. Back in the old days, one tended to rely upon one's intuition about somebody. I hope she saw that deep inside I was, more or less, a passably honest person.

"Ma'am," I might have said. "There are certain people in my life who have done me much harm. And God knows I've done my share of terrible things in this world. Maybe forgiving others is just an acknowledgment that we see ourselves in them, that we, too, are capable of committing their crimes. I could be wrong, ma'am, but forgiveness might just be a form of putting oneself in another person's shoes."

But coming up with such wisdom spontaneously was never my forte. I'm always late to the party. And now that I think about it, the reference to shoes might throw Mrs. Aquino off, considering whom we were about to visit. Or perhaps I might make her laugh inadvertently, which could be a good thing. You see what I mean. I take too long to think and I second-guess myself.

It is possible that I would finally have opened up about you. I've always wanted to, you know. But it has never been easy. And with each missed opportunity, the impulse to go back in time becomes harder and harder to justify.

You gave me that chance, once.

I'm talking, of course, about the letter you sent me many, many years ago. You were still in high school, but you said that your classmates had already started planning for college. This was why you wrote to me. You had just found out that you weren't qualified for your government's financial aid, because they couldn't find your name in the documents where it was supposed to appear. You and your mother technically didn't exist in the U.S.

I can only imagine how hard that must've been for you. How angry you were at your mother for hiding this terrible secret. All this time you thought you were just another immigrant kid on the block. You'd lost your ability to speak Tagalog, you said in your letter. But, like many other Filipinos in America, you could still understand it. Over the years, you said, you'd never once stopped to question the things your mother had told you. When she said that you couldn't get a summer job because you had to take piano lessons, you accepted it. During spring break of your freshman year, your friend's family invited you to go to Costa Rica. Your mother told you that you couldn't go, because money was tight. And when your friend offered to pay your part, your mother said, "What do they think we are? A charity case?" You were baffled by her reaction, but still, you never suspected her. And finally, when it came to me—your biological father— you were told about my true identity and how we got separated, that I had "a very important job" working for "a very important person" in the Philippines. That was why I had to stay here, she said. How the story evolved to fit the changing circumstances as you grew up, I will never know. I imagine that the topic of your long-neglectful father was not a favorite one at the dinner table.

But I was resurrected after you found out about your legal status. Suddenly, at sixteen, you were trying to reconnect with me. You said in your letter that you had some faint memories of us together. You told me of a time when we were at an arcade in Manila, one with lots of neon lights. After playing a round of hoops, you intended to exchange the prize tickets for some cotton candy. But some other boy swiped them away when you weren't paying attention. You pointed him out to me. The boy wasn't much older than you, you wrote, but he was bigger. When I confronted him, the fool ran to his father, and then both of them denied the theft of the tickets. I expected that you'd tell me how I'd fought them bravely and saved the day. But no, the story ended right there.

To be honest, I don't remember this whole episode. But being bullied does seem to fit what it means to be a man in our family. So it felt true enough, and it broke my heart to pieces.

———————

After I'd received and read your letter back then, for a few days I could think of nothing else. You hadn't quite said that you wanted me to intercede on your behalf. But I felt it was implied. Of course, I don't think you knew then what kind of job I really had, how little ability I possessed to request such a favor.

Still, I thought I could try. Mrs. Aquino had powerful friends in the Department of Foreign Affairs and even in the U.S. government, no doubt. It was just a matter of principle, and, for me, of extreme discomfort. How far would she go to do a good turn for her driver's long-lost son? And what would she think of me for even asking? I hoped that it could be the kind of thing that involved a simple call to a lower-level officer. I had no real idea of how citizenship was given out. It seemed to me like it should be granted to a person if he truly wanted it and worked hard for it. But I guess I was talking myself into thinking I could help you.

I chose a morning in December, when the climate tends to be cooler, when everyone is preparing for Christmas and feeling a little more generous. I remember I was driving the Mercedes, listening to the radio, on my way to the palace to fetch Mrs. Aquino. I was rehearsing in my mind how I could tell your story as delicately as possible.

That was when I heard the news of a coup. A convoy of trucks had gotten inside the presidential compound, and some armed men wearing ski masks had flung mortars and grenades. The rebels had also taken over the airport and some air bases near the capital. I could get only as close as to the Quezon Bridge before traffic hit a standstill. In the distance I thought I could make out the sound of rapid gunfire. I wanted to charge through the blockade and then to the palace, but at the same time I wanted to stay the hell out of it. Nobody was responding to my questions on the two-way radio. I began to worry about Mrs. Aquino.

While I waited for news, the thought came to me that the rebels might have something to do with the Communist Party. By that time it had been more than a decade since I'd lived in the mountains with my father. And even though there were a few different Communist factions—some more local than others—all of them wanted a revolution. I always worried that if anyone found out about my past, I'd be suspected of being an enemy plant, plotting to harm the president. Nothing could be further from the truth, of course. But the truth is not always so apparent.

The radio announcer interrupted the program to say that Mrs. Aquino had telephoned in to deliver a live broadcast. Her voice came through, somewhat hoarse, if not a bit shaken. "I want to tell you, all my countrymen, that I am safe." I sighed. "It's all right here," she said, "but it's a little noisy." The understatement was very typical of her and made me smile.

By the end of that day, the coup had been quelled. Close to three hundred people were injured or had died, among them three of the bodyguards assigned to Mrs. Aquino's son, who were killed while protecting him. He was seriously wounded himself, though he eventually recovered. Other things came to light: Mrs. Aquino, it turned out, had called the United States. She'd asked for help and they sent some fighter planes from Clark Air Base to retake the airport. She was severely criticized for this show of weakness.

Needless to say, I never did talk to Mrs. Aquino about you, not on that day, or on any other. I guess the matter must have felt very trivial compared to everything else that was happening.

I don't mean to say that you were trivial to me. I wish that I could've helped you. And I am most sorry that I did not.

Milo is back, looking none the worse for wear. And guess what else the cat dragged in with him this morning? Milo promptly excused himself to leave me alone with my visitor. But I told him I wasn't done with him yet. He and I were to talk later, I said, and he promised that we would.

"So it's you again, huh?" I said to my visitor.

"Afraid so." Manang Dionisia shut the door and drew up a chair right next to me. Then she took out from her basket a sandwich wrapped in cellophane. She said, "It's your favorite."

"A sandwich?"

"Pork knuckle stew in sweet sauce. I've shredded the meat and tucked it between the bread. So if anyone asks, we tell them it's chicken salad."

I looked at her morosely. Then I started laughing. It was as close to an apology for calling me a coward as I'd get from that woman.

"I see you're behaving yourself now," she said. "Even getting along with the nurse, it seems? Miracles, indeed."

"I don't recall any misbehavior," I said, peeling the wrapper off the sandwich. "Anyway, Milo's not so bad, once you get to know him."

"Mm-hmm," she said, but stopped herself. "How is your"— she looked down at her dress, as if reading from a script—"your son?"

Fine, I said. I told her that we'd been talking. Or rather,

I said that I'd been talking *to* you. I didn't make the emphasis strong, and I don't think she caught the difference. I bit into the bread.

"How old is he, by the way? Forties?"

"Forty-one," I said. "This coming May. A good age to be."

"Right," she said.

"This is really something," I said, pointing to the sandwich. "You've outdone yourself."

"Perhaps that says more about the food here than my cooking."

"There's truth to that."

"Anyway," she said, "the reason I'm asking—"

"What did you do to the meat?" I asked. "Aside from pressurizing it, which I know you did, because I've always seen you tinkering with that hissing device. But is there something else? It's as if all the flavors are packed inside the fibers, as if they'd been injected with the marinade. Is that it? Did you inject the meat first?"

"No, I just let it soak in lime for a few hours," she said. "That breaks down the meat."

"Really, just lime? For a few hours? I should try that myself when I get home."

"Have you considered that there might not be a home to return to?" Manang Dionisia was clever enough to seize upon the opening I'd given her by accident. "Lito, I've spoken with your doctors."

"I see."

"Your kidneys are failing. They said your heart attack has damaged them permanently. Eventually you'll have to use the machines here to clean your body for the rest of your life. Do you know what that means? If you miss just one cleaning, you'll bloat from the poison in your blood and die."

"It's called dialysis," I said.

She nodded. "I don't want you to misunderstand me," she said. "They—the people who've been maintaining your care— they support you all the way. Money's not an issue. The only thing we want is what's best for you."

She was talking, of course, about Mrs. Aquino's children, whom I've always suspected of paying my hospital bills, and now for the treatment. The shift from *they* to *we* was subtle but nevertheless made me uncomfortable. I'd lost my appetite, and I placed the food on the table.

"I'm tired," I said. "I haven't been sleeping well."

"I understand that it's hard. But can you just think about it?" she asked. "A kidney transplant would be the better solution. He is your only living relation, Lito. And they said it wouldn't do him any harm, either."

Yesterday, right before I went to bed, I realized that I'd written something stupid, something that could easily be taken out of context. The whole narrative about the pork sandwich was funny in my mind, before I realized too late that it was headed in the wrong direction. Of course, I had to finish the story by then, or you'd have wondered what I was leaving out.

Son, I am very upset with myself.

I've gotten dangerously used to this. That is, telling you everything without first filtering my thoughts. Partly it's this situation I'm in, where simply pushing pen against the paper takes up all my energy. I have none left for editing or rethinking. I'm not complaining. Like I said, I've gotten used to it. But you'll just have to deal with my occasional slipups.

I don't know when my letters will reach you and I doubt I'll still be alive by then. But on the off chance that I'm still breathing, please do not think that I have any motive other than to tell you a good story. I will never, ever ask you to give me what belongs to you, son. I could never live with myself if I knew that a part of me was taken from a part of you. Even if you were to offer it to me on a golden plate, or tie it with a pretty ribbon, I swear I'd burn the whole thing up. Your mother and I gave you all your organs, and inside you is where they'll stay forever.

There. I hope I've made myself abundantly clear. We shall never speak of this again.

———

You know, I have often thought of death.

And I don't say this to get a reaction from you. It's just a statement of fact. I have often thought of death because I believe it is the only way to prepare for it. Am I afraid of the prospect of suddenly not existing? Of course. One wouldn't be human if one never pondered that possibility. But what I eventually learned about fears is this: the only way to overcome them is through practice. That's why, sometimes when I have the chance, like when I'm lining up at the grocery checkout, or having my hair cut—what's left of it, anyway—or standing at the water refilling station, I imagine the many different scenarios in which I might take my last breath. That way, when the day finally arrives, it will be as if I've rehearsed it all along. I won't be caught off guard. I'll accept my death calmly and with some relief, having awaited the moment for a long time.

By the way, I am no stranger to the foibles of a dying father. Nor have I forgotten that I owe you the final act of the epic journey I once undertook with my father. Now, as I sit here alone, the bed reclined and the pillows softly propping me up, I believe it's as good a time as any to bring that story to a close.

———

After my breakdown inside Ka Anna's hut—for what else but a breakdown would you call talking to oneself and plotting to burn a man alive?—I returned to live in the lowlands. Actually, from then on I ceased to think in terms of a "low" and a "high" land. That kind of differentiation is useful only when one is trying to pass relative judgment on things, and at that time I preferred not to make any comparisons. I was desperate to erase all of my memories of that strange year in that strange place.

And I was successful, more or less. I had known from the beginning that I did not want to go back to Moncada. I wanted to start fresh, to have as little as possible to do with who I'd been and what I'd gone through. But I did not have the means. I needed money, and the only person who could help me was my father, who was not pleased with what he thought of as my desertion.

So I took my chances and made for the nearest big city, which happened to be Tarlac. There my savings would barely last me three days, even though I stayed in the cheapest dormitory I could find. It was the smelliest and foulest place I've ever lived in, and possibly that ever existed on the face of the earth.

Looking back, I can see that I was very foolish, and I could easily have gotten myself into trouble—contracted some fatal disease or perhaps gotten kidnapped and shipped off to do forced labor. None of that came to pass, thankfully. But after three whole days of answering newspaper ads and flyers, going door-to-door and talking to store managers, I was not able to land myself any jobs.

Perhaps everyone saw through my lies about my age. Or perhaps they simply didn't have suitable positions for me. Because what skills did I have back then? Gardening? Reciting poems? Spewing Marxist philosophy? And I already had my doubts about that last one.

On the afternoon of the third day, as I leaned against a lamppost outside an old marketplace, I knew that only a miracle would save me from joining the masses that faced starvation every day. Even the pigeon that had come to peck at the remnants of some spilled rice could boast of something to eat. I remember thinking of that girl in the story who tries to sell matchsticks in the middle of winter, and when she fails to do so, must light them one by one for warmth.

In contrast, of course, it was very hot where I lay down. I could feel the burning concrete through my pants. I was quite sure I would pass out. I put my hands in my pockets and held on to my wallet. There, I felt the damp leather and the bumpy ridges of the trim. I felt the stitches going in and out, holding the folds together and protecting the contents. But what contents? At that point the wallet itself was the most precious item I owned! I almost cried at the absurdity of it. That was when it suddenly came to me. From the ID case I took out a piece of yellowed paper, which, for no other reason than sheer habit and laziness, I had

kept with me all these years. On it I could still make out the faint
scribbles of a child's handwriting, with digits that corresponded
to the phone number of my father's sister.

———————

Once more I threw myself upon her mercy, and once more did she
come to my rescue. This time around, however, she asked very few
questions, I suppose because she recognized that I had become
an adult. Or maybe it was my squalor that convinced her to go
easy on me. She doused my hair and neck with some thick yellow
liquid. Then she took me to a barber and instructed him to shave
my head clean. I guess she suspected that I had lice, which, most
likely, I did. But the effect was like that of baptism, at once purg-
ing and restoring me. As soon as we got back to her house and I
hit the couch, I slept like a baby.

I didn't know how much taller and leaner I had become until
I studied myself in the mirror the next morning. I wouldn't say
that I was thin, exactly, but certainly the thinnest I had ever been.
My growth spurt had kicked in while I was up in the mountains and carrying out all that manual work. I must've consumed
everything that my aunt put on the table, and still she didn't ask
for any details about my life or my father. I think she was a wise
woman. She had a mother's instincts, though she never had any
children of her own, whether by choice or by circumstance.

"You told me you were looking for a job," she said. I nodded.

"I know someone who needs help on a part-time basis. An
old matriarch," she said, "but she has very high expectations. Can
you drive?"

I said that I could not.

She shook her head. "Then what are you waiting for? Do you think you'll learn how to drive just lying there on the couch?"

"No, ma'am," I said.

The very same day, my aunt sat me in the driver's seat and herself on the passenger side of her Type 1 Beetle and started teaching me everything there was to know about driving, or at least what she knew of it. We spent several days in that car, which I'll always remember—it led me to believe that all cars had their engines installed at the back. In any case, we started by fumbling around the church parking lot, then progressed to the barangay roads, where I learned how to back up and pull U-turns. I couldn't parallel park until much later, but as soon as I managed to drive without any supervision, that was enough for my aunt to bring me to the nearest LTO to get myself a license.

She then phoned her friend to set me up for the interview. It turned out that the friend had been stalling for me, on my aunt's request, so I could have the first—and hopefully final—shot at the job. When my aunt and I arrived outside the gate of the old house, her friend greeted me.

"So this is him," she said. "Still a bit wet behind the ears, I see. But he might do."

"Lito," my aunt said, "this is my best friend, Dionisia. Please always mind your manners and only call her Manang Dionisia."

———

I trust you already know what happened next. Doña Aurora hired me on the spot. But I only worked for her for less than a year, because I found out that her son and his wife, who visited often from Manila, were in search of a family driver. I took the first chance that came my way to move to a real city. Sometime later, your mother was hired as a cleaning maid for the old woman. But she soon followed in my footsteps, and moved to Manila as a nanny.

I did not hear from or about my father for quite a while. One day, out of the blue, my aunt showed up in Manila and told me to go and see him as soon as I could. She wouldn't tell me why, only that he was back in Moncada, living by himself in a ramshackle apartment.

"Don't let this chance pass you by," she said. "You might regret it forever."

As far as I was concerned, that was unlikely. I barely thought of my father anymore, and perhaps it was seeing him that would fill me with regret. Still, I thanked her for telling me, and said that I'd think about it.

"This isn't a time for thinking," she said, "but for just going." When I continued to resist, she said, "Do it for me."

I consented. I took her out to dinner that night before she left. Even though I had made the promise, I hadn't given her a timeline, so I sat on it. I was also really busy in those days. Remember, I was attending classes as well as driving. Mrs. Aquino had discovered that I'd never graduated, and she wanted me to at least earn a high school diploma, in case I wanted to go to college later on. She said, "I can tell you have a good mind, Lito. Don't waste it. Unless you want to be a driver for the rest of your life."

Funny how that one turned out.

When I wasn't driving or studying, there was your mother.

Now, I don't mean to lump her in with my other chores. In fact, seeing her used to be the highlight of my week. In any case, it was on one of our days off, a Saturday, when your mother and I went out to breakfast together. We were at a diner when I came across the article in a newspaper. It was rather short, and fell somewhere in the middle pages. But my eye was drawn to a photo of a familiar face, above a caption with an unfamiliar name. The man was identified as a former priest and a rebel leader. He had been arrested and was awaiting trial. The charges included sedition, fraud, drug possession, embezzlement, and racketeering.

At the time I did not fully understand those terms, but I knew that they were serious crimes with serious punishments. I must've looked distracted, because I remember your mother asking me what was wrong. I said nothing, of course, and immediately folded the paper away, setting it out of her reach. We then went to watch a movie as we'd planned. But throughout that hour and a half, I could not concentrate. I kept thinking about the piece of news that I'd read. I wondered when it had happened, and if my father was also in trouble. I kept seeing him, and Ka Noel, in the fleeting images of that dark space.

When we left the cinema, your mother stopped me. She said, "Clearly there's something going on with you." I brushed it off again but she stood her ground. "We're not going home until you tell me." I was a bit irritated at her for this, because she was usually very patient, a trait that I greatly admired. I tried to hold her hand but she retracted it. "Tell me!" she said, almost shouting.

"Okay," I said. I did not want to cause a scene. "But can we go somewhere else?"

We spent the rest of the afternoon in a park, where, under the cover of trees, I tried my best to answer all of her questions. My initial embarrassment turned into anger and then anxiety, before I felt some amount of relief and even of gratitude. Here, at last, was someone, I thought, who cared enough about me to listen. And she didn't once judge me for my past.

I went to see my father about a month later. The address that my aunt had given me led me to a government housing block in Moncada. The buildings all looked the same, and unfinished, as if construction had been halted halfway through because of shifting priorities. Or perhaps the contractor disappeared and ran away with the money.

My father opened the door and asked me to come in. He even inquired whether I had eaten lunch yet. It was oddly normal, as if he'd been expecting me all along, or we still lived with each other. At first glance, he also looked exactly like he had the last time I saw him, neither older nor thinner. He wore his hair straight back, and the smell of pomade permeated everything he touched. At the same time, I sensed there was something different about him, though I couldn't be sure at first what it was. It took a couple of visits before we managed to talk beyond the usual pleasantries.

One day while visiting, I brought him a bag of star bread so we could have breakfast together. I poured him a glass of powdered milk, and, because I was feeling fine that morning, I asked him to tell me about what happened after I left the mountains.

"Everything," my father said, his eyes growing big. "You missed everything."

He went on to tell me about how he had helped Ka Noel and his men recruit in Santo Tomas, Gerona, and even back in Moncada. My father was the one who introduced them to the town's businessmen, who were initially skeptical of the movement. "But you should see how Ka Noel won them over. He spoke to them one by one, on their own terms. By the end of our mission, all the townspeople, rich and poor, were on our side. I guess he just told them the truth about what's happening to our country. How it's in everyone's interest to have real equality, where everyone's given a real chance to succeed in life—good education, a good house, a good job. We've had so many leaders in this country already, and they're all the same, they're all just looking out for themselves and their friends. Even this new one, this Aquino, is no different. What we need is a real revolution to change things. From someone who understands because he's always been with the people. Ka Noel."

"Is that right?" I said.

"Don't buy in to what they say," my father said. "I know he's been on the news lately. But the news isn't always true."

Without prompting, my father went on to talk about the court trial. He said the police had tortured the witnesses and had made them sign confessions to ensure that the trial went the way they wanted. "Even so, Ka Noel only treated them with respect and kindness. He even helped one of the officers' kids who had mumps. The boy's face looked hot and red and about ready to fall off on one side. But the next day, he was completely fine, licking an iced Popsicle. One touch from Ka Noel—that was all it took!"

"I can't believe you're still so blinded by him," I said, throwing down the bag of bread. "Don't you see that he was just using you and everybody else to get what he wanted?"

"I was there and I saw it with my own eyes!"

"Of course, that's the work of a con man."

"Stop talking about things you don't understand."

"I understand perfectly, Father," I said. "I understand he's a hypocrite."

My father seemed pained by this, as if I had accused him directly. A hypocrite was the worst thing you could call a person, at least in my father's opinion.

"Look where he is now," I said. "In jail. Where he belongs."

"You're wrong about this," he said.

"I hope he spends a lot of sleepless nights there."

"It was my fault," my father said. "I betrayed him."

He said that Ka Noel's men stuck together, even under threat of more torture. They didn't cooperate with the police's plan to frame Ka Noel in exchange for their freedom. It was proof of their strong conviction, my father said. But then, one day, Ka Noel instructed them all to give in. He told them that they would be of no use if they rotted away in prison. He commanded them to make up lies about him so the others could go back to the mountains and continue with the cause. But now that my father was free again, he said, he was too tired and too afraid to go back.

"It's funny you keep mentioning freedom," I said. "Because people like Ka Noel, they only appeal to those who secretly want to give up their freedom. They demand complete obedience, and I can see that you've willingly submitted. You don't want to admit it, Father, but being free can be exhausting. Having to make choices for yourself and face the consequences of your actions can be exhausting. Having to constantly think for yourself can be exhausting. So you offer up your mind and soul to this one magical man so that he can take charge of your life."

"That's not true," my father shouted, and with his cry a dollop of blood came spilling out of his mouth.

I felt as if I had caused it. As if his lifelong habit of binge drinking had nothing to do with the sickness already lurking inside, as if his liver were pristine until the moment I pierced it with my spiteful words. And even if I could accept that he'd already been a bit pale and yellowish when I walked through his door, I felt that my visit had only sapped him further.

He stopped talking to me after that day.

As his health deteriorated over the following years, I visited him more and more. I eventually quit school so I could be with him every weekend. Even at the height of martial law, after you and your mother left for the United States with the Aquinos, I braved checkpoints and curfews just to make my way to Moncada. My father was barely clinging to life then, rather like the country itself at the time.

I must admit that the matter of Ka Noel remains unsettled with me. I did hurl many accusations at my father, but you have to understand that some of what I said had little to do with the truth. I wanted to hurt my father, and seeing him weak and pitiful only fueled my desire.

In any case, I still wonder sometimes if Ka Noel was the person he claimed to be. Though I could think of a few practical explanations for the supposed miracles he'd performed, I also don't discount the possibility that some of them might have been real. In this, as with the issue of God, I suppose you could consider me an agnostic.

Whatever happened to the black trunk in Ka Noel's hut? I think the answer to many of the mysteries surrounding him could have been found inside. He told me something magical was hidden inside the trunk, something I should fear. Was Ka Noel such a trickster that even in his sleep he was able to lie so well?

The story of Pandora's box, of course, comes to mind. My father told me that tale when I was a child. It's among the very few good memories I have of him: he sitting at the edge of my bed, smoking a cigarette, and I in my pajamas, lying facedown like a starfish. I would flail my arms when I heard about misfortunes, such as when Zeus tied up Prometheus for stealing fire from the gods and giving it to humans. I'd smile and turn around when the stories were happier, like the one about the creation of beautiful Pandora and of her marriage to Epimetheus. At the end of most of these stories, my father would tidily sum up the lessons they offered. But I remember there was something different about this myth, which he told me several times, each time with a new moral. Once, he said something like "This teaches us about the consequences of human actions." And once, because Pandora released all kinds of chaos into the world when she opened the forbidden box: "Disobedience always leads to trouble." But there was a moment, too, when he was still finishing the story, and we came to the part about Pandora closing the box and trapping the last thing inside, when my father paused to collect his thoughts.

"That's a sad ending," I said. "Why was Hope inside, and why didn't Pandora choose to release it?"

"I don't think she knew," he said. He paused, and then he told me something I didn't quite understand at the time. My father said, "Even if Pandora did know what she was holding, perhaps that makes for a rather good ending. It means she saved us all by sealing inside the worst of human afflictions: hope."

———————

My father died on a quiet Friday morning in April 1987. This was during Mrs. Aquino's first year in office. I knew I'd have a hard time taking off work without good reason, but I did not want to tell anyone about my father. Rather than lie, I decided to say nothing at all. I simply disappeared for a week. And if they wouldn't take me back, I thought, then so be it.

He refused to be admitted to a hospital. He preferred to die alone, said my aunt, and if she'd called me any later, he'd have gotten his wish. I arrived by bus on a Tuesday night. Right away I could see what she had meant when she told me to go as soon as I could: my father had shriveled up and hardly resembled his old self. He was slumped against the doorway for support. He had no reason to be presentable, so everything that he could let hang was doing so. He wore a shirt that was too big for him. His hair was long and greasy. He wasn't even wearing any pants. I covered him up with a blanket and eased him onto the bed.

The whole first day I was there, he didn't say anything. When he woke up, I knew that I had to carry him to the bathroom. He never asked for anything to eat. I fed him rice gruel, sprinkling it with sugar so he'd open his mouth. I stayed by his side, reading a book out loud. I thought the sound of someone's voice would soothe him and remind him I was there if he needed me.

On Thursday morning, I got up and saw that his bed was empty. I was afraid he might have fallen somewhere, but instead I found him in the kitchen, cooking some eggs. He still looked messy, but cheerfully so, and I thought he might even recover. He asked me to take a seat. And then he told me that he'd seen Ka Noel in his dream.

"There was a thunderstorm. And mud water was pouring in everywhere, through these walls, the door, and even the roof. We were both sleeping inside my room, but we were safe and dry. Ka Noel was with us. He was protecting us."

"You had a nightmare," I said.

"It wasn't a nightmare," my father said. "It was a good dream and a good reminder." He sighed. "I've never told you this, but right after your mother died, I often thought of ending my own life. Each time I went out and left you by yourself, I thought I might never return."

"Somehow I knew that," I said.

"Did you also know that I didn't like your mother?"

I admit I didn't expect him to say that, but given how sick he was, I wasn't surprised that he'd started to become confused. He didn't even look at me, but continued to stir the pan.

"It's true," he said. "If you ever wondered why I never told you much about her when you were growing up, it's because she was seldom on my mind. She was somebody convenient. That was all."

"Then why did you go to the trouble of hunting down Ka Noel?"

"You're not understanding me," he said. "Yes, I admit I was angry, at first. I wanted revenge. It's a man's instinct to fight back, when something or someone is taken away from him. Then it became guilt, because I took her for granted. Like I said, she was seldom on my mind. But the more time passed, the more I missed her. I didn't realize just how much I loved her until she was no longer around." He turned off the heat and set the pan aside. "When we were in the mountains, Ka Noel helped me see that. He saved me, son. I hope you can acknowledge that. He saved both of us."

I said nothing. And then he sat down in front of me and made that impossible request.

"People are going to say things," my father said. "They're going to lie and accuse him of many things, because it's the way of the world. I did this, too, and I was selfish and wrong. So you have to promise me that no matter what happens, you're not going to make the same mistake I did. Promise me, my son, that you're not going to turn against Ka Noel. Not ever."

I said I could not make such a vow.

He repeated himself, more upset each time, until tears fell down his cheeks.

I want to tell you something about myself that is difficult for me to express. I still haven't figured out the right way to do this, except that I've thought about it not a few times now and I've decided it's best to get it over with. You see, I've tried to keep certain things out of our story as much as I could. Maybe it's because I don't see the relevance of including details of my private life and such—I feel I've already told you too much about myself. I'm sorry about that. I'm sure you're not interested. But at the risk of further taxing your patience, I think I'll go ahead with it. I must go ahead with it. And I'll try to be brief.

When I was at the boarding school, I did in fact have a friend. Ramon—he was the roommate I was telling you about, the consummate snorer. One good thing about Ramon was that he used to wake up every morning at six, on the dot, as if he had a built-in alarm clock. He was also generous, and he'd share his food with me—canned corned beef and Vienna sausages that his family always sent him. Those, over rice, used to be our staple breakfast. We'd also walk to campus together and never missed a flag ceremony. We'd become known as the duo, one short and the other tall, who were never late to class. On my first Christmas there, Ramon asked where I would be spending the holiday. When he found out that I had planned to stay at the boarding school, because my father told me not to expect him back so soon, Ramon took pity on me. He asked his parents if he could bring me home with him, and they agreed. This became a series of invitations, not just for Christmas, but also for Holy Week, summer break, semester break, then the following Christmas again, and so forth. He became the brother I never had. I grew quite close to him. One day, during intramurals, Ramon asked me if I fancied any girl at school, and when I said I didn't particularly like anyone, he said he'd been curious what they would feel like. What? I asked. Breasts, he said. It's the awesomest thing there is, according to some boys. But we weren't very popular. Girls wouldn't give us the time of day. So Ramon asked me—I remember we were in the shower, all sweaty, having just returned from basketball, which we were both bad at—he asked me if he could touch my breasts. "Stop being weird," I said. But he was serious, he said, he was just curious what it would feel like, you know, the real thing, and would I just let him, once, so that he could tell the boys that he'd actually touched one, don't worry about whose? I don't know why I let him. And, more important, I don't know why he told the boys afterward that he did touch mine, that it was all droopy and no different from a girl's. I don't actually think Ramon meant any harm. I don't think he meant to hurt me. I think he was just being honest. But the boys took it and ran with it. They made me new nicknames, which I don't need to repeat here, and they taunted not only me, but, of course, Ramon, too. That's when he started to despise me. I told you that I was pudgy back then. I'm sure it was somewhat accurate that I did have breasts like a girl's. Ramon was just stating a fact. I knew, too, that I was undesirable. And so when Ka Noel paid attention to me in a certain way, I didn't know how to respond. At first it felt like I had a lot of power and control, but that shifted. I hated myself for it and I never wanted to tell a soul about what happened. Your mother, in fact, is the only one who knows everything about me. She once said that I should come clean. I could save others from Ka Noel, she said. They didn't need to become like me, their futures forever ruined by one man.

It was unjust of my father to ask me to make a vow about Ka Noel. I think he knew this. But on his face I could see so much suffering and pain and desperation. He was convinced it was the right thing to do, because new allegations had been surfacing about Ka Noel. I don't know why it is, but even intelligent people often fail to understand that a person can be capable of doing both many good deeds and many evil ones. Calling the person out for his crimes isn't a betrayal. Rather, it offers him a path to redemption.

But no matter how I thought about it, the fact remained that he was my father, and it was impossible to change his mind. I pitied him in his state. He was never the perfect father, far from it, but I was also never the perfect son. So when he pleaded again, with tears in his eyes, I finally gave him my word. My father slouched in his chair, as if draping his weary bones for the last time, and then he became quiet.

There is a question I've never put to anybody. And here I am going to ask you now. Was what I did cowardly, or was it an act of kindness? Did I compromise my own dignity and allow Ka Noel to escape a measure of justice? Or did I show my father the right kind of compassion and mercy and love?

I wish you would tell me. I wish you could talk to me, son. I guess you are still unhappy about everything that's happened to you because of me, and I shall bear that mark for the rest of my life. Maybe I deserve it. Or maybe you're being too harsh to your own father.

One thing is for sure. To this day, I have never said an ill word about Ka Noel. For better or worse, I have kept that promise to my father. And I intend to see it through.

10

IT WAS DUSK when we approached the entrance to the mountain range surrounding Baguio. I had taken the longer route, because I feared Kennon Road might be prone to landslides at that time of the year, especially because it had recently rained. Agoo Road was wider and better paved, though some parts of it were also steeper. I trusted that the Crown was ready for it.

We had long since passed the point of no return, Mrs. Aquino and I, but crossing these mountains felt like the final hurdle. I'd always tried to avoid driving through them at night. Those mountains are what come to mind whenever I hear the verse "Though I walk through the valley of the shadow of death." It's a different story during the day, of course, with the view of the coastline on one side, and vendors selling fruits and souvenirs on the other. There was still some sunlight left, then, and I intended to reach the summit before it was completely washed in darkness.

Agoo Road has another name, you might be interested to learn. For a long time, it was known as the Marcos Highway. In fact, many people still call it that—not, I think, out of any particular allegiance to the former president, although there's certainly more of that going around these days. People have short memories. Anyway, there used to be a landmark around these parts: the oversize bust of Mr. Marcos cast in concrete. He looked down at you as you drove up the road to the mountain range. It was hard to miss. But during the eighties, Communist rebels were said to have destroyed it. Others blamed treasure hunters. They apparently placed dynamite around Mr. Marcos's neck, hoping to unearth any gold bars hidden underneath. Who knows if that's true? What's certain is that no trace of the concrete statue remains.

You have been there, by the way, believe it or not, and I have the picture at home to prove it. That was a special picture, too. Because it might be the only one with all of us together—you, your mother, and I, and even the Aquinos, standing in a parking lot with the giant face in the backdrop. Mr. Aquino was not there, as he was still locked up at the army camp. The trip to Baguio was supposed to give the children some sort of respite from all the stress of the politics happening in the capital. But the Marcoses seemed omnipresent. That particular bust, when we drove toward it, seemed to be waiting there especially to torment us. This did not deter you, curious child that you were, from asking to see it up close.

"Maybe on our way back," I said, hoping by then you'd find something else to occupy yourself with. But no. You insisted on seeing it that very moment, punctuating your point with some theatrical tears.

"Oh my God, will you shut up?" said her youngest daughter.

"Language," said Mrs. Aquino. She was looking for a tissue with which to wipe your face.

I felt bad for her, not only for the awkwardness of the

situation, but for the pain she had to conceal from the children. I was sure she was thinking of her husband, and perhaps wondering if it was such a good idea to be leaving town while he was alone and suffering. I'm not saying that I blame you, of course. You were four years old at the time. You were filling the role any child that age is meant to play.

Mrs. Aquino came up with a shrewd compromise. Before we all got out of the van, she told us we'd use the opportunity to reflect on dictatorships and what happens when people's rights are taken away. She gave each of you some time to think about it.

Once we got down, we asked a stranger to take the picture. At the count of three, we all raised our hands with our index finger and thumb sticking out. That L was supposed to stand for "Laban," or "Fight." I believe it was the first time the sign was ever used, and nobody around us knew any better. So we got away with our little act of insurrection.

Perhaps you can remind me to send the picture to you. It might come in handy someday, if you want to tell the story. But I'm merely suggesting, not insisting. As I've said before, what you want to do with this story is completely up to you. You think on what's best for you now. You decide.

"Welcome to Baguio," I said. "Ma'am, we've finally made it."

"Yes, I can read the sign," said Mrs. Aquino. Ahead of us, a big arch reading SUMMER CAPITAL, CITY OF BAGUIO spanned the roadway. "But thank you, Lito. It's a miracle."

I could've reminded her that the Crown did break down on us halfway through. If miracles had been in play, the radiator should've fixed itself, or somehow the old car should have held itself together until we arrived. But I let it slide. It had been a long day for both of us.

"Look," Mrs. Aquino said. "Fresh strawberries!"

As if she'd uttered the magic words, the streetlights lit up. It was a sight to behold, the crates of fruits and flowers and vegetables displayed on the sidewalk, coated with a layer of mist, as if we were driving through the refrigerated aisle in a supermarket. I could see why the Americans had loved Baguio, how the climate had reminded them of home, and why they went to the trouble of building much of the city.

"We used to bring the kids here," Mrs. Aquino said as we passed the willow trees of Burnham Park. "Do you remember the carousel rides and the bumper cars? Kris especially enjoyed the swan boats. Do you see them, Lito? The boats are still there."

"I see them," I said, thinking about a particular boy who also used to like to ride the boats, greedily munching on his peanut brittle all the while.

"I never thought I'd come back here," Mrs. Aquino said.

"I never thought I'd be back here, either," I said.

It occurred to me then that it was unlikely that Mrs. Aquino would go on another long journey. After this, she might be confined to her own house in Manila for the rest of her days. And I think the thought also occurred to her. We shared a moment of silence.

A muffled ringing came from somewhere in the backseat, then grew louder and sharper as Mrs. Aquino found her purse and opened it.

"Hello," she said. "Hello? Can you hear me?"

I heard a beep and then her sigh.

"The phone died," she said. "I forgot to charge it earlier."

"Do you want me to turn the car around?" I joked. "There's still time to go back, ma'am."

"No," she said. "I must go on with this."

"Very well, ma'am."

We stopped at the intersection, where a charity group's billboard sat on an island next to their iconic yellow cog. I had seen many of their advertisements before, but never had I paid as much attention to one as I did then. THE FOUR-WAY TEST, the sign proclaimed, with the following sentences:

1. IS IT THE TRUTH?
2. IS IT FAIR TO ALL CONCERNED?
3. WILL IT BUILD GOODWILL AND BETTER FRIENDSHIPS?
4. WILL IT BE BENEFICIAL TO ALL CONCERNED?

Tests are sometimes a good way to overcome our own biases, forcing us to be more honest with ourselves. Of course, they're only as good as our sincerity in coming up with real answers. In my mind I substituted "it" with "forgiving Imelda Marcos." Such as, "Is forgiving Imelda Marcos the Truth?" That first question was rather awkwardly phrased, I admit. But I thought it had more to do with facts—forgiving her would become true in just a matter of minutes or a few hours, depending on how the talk between Mrs. Aquino and Mrs. Marcos transpired. "Will forgiving Imelda Marcos be Fair to all concerned?" The Aquino children would probably have a very negative answer to that one. But because Mrs. Aquino was the head of the family, her decision wouldn't be seen as merely personal. It would carry the full force of the entire clan. Her forgiveness, I thought, would practically and inevitably mean that all Aquinos would have also forgiven Imelda Marcos in the eyes of the public. "Will that build Goodwill and Better Friendships?" Not if it was premature. In fact, it would likely create even more discord among the Aquinos—not to mention many Filipinos, especially victims of martial law, who might feel betrayed. Those who stood up for Mrs. Aquino because she stood for fairness, freedom, and transparency—what would happen if that icon of democracy herself decided to let go of the past? And here was the biggest problem: the answer to the fourth and last question, "Will it be Beneficial to all concerned?" I thought long and hard before concluding that only Mrs. Aquino would likely benefit from forgiving Imelda Marcos. It would be cathartic for her. But even the Marcoses, whose political and social standing might be elevated by Mrs. Aquino's act, would deny deriving any benefit. Because they'd deny the need to be forgiven in the first place, having always denied any wrongdoing, and never having demonstrated any kind of remorse or contrition or humility.

I hoped that Mrs. Aquino had seen the billboard so she, too, could ponder its questions for herself. But when I checked the rearview mirror, I saw that she was applying makeup and had already taken off her scarf.

———

The house on Poblete Street was long and symmetrical. Even in the night, I could see that every inch of it was painted in different shades of pink. Gables framed each roof, and on each triangle two sets of lights were turned on to display a rectangular window. The whole thing looked to me like a giant dollhouse, or a child's idea of a fancy birthday cake. A driveway unfurled toward us from the center, with trees and some well-behaved shrubbery dotting both sides. Barring us from entry was a black iron gate with iron curls that reminded me of a peacock's tail. The gate was as dainty as a tiara. The house seemed to want to be seen, but mostly to be admired from a distance.

"I've no doubt this is the right place," I said, pulling the hand brake.

"Yes, it is," Mrs. Aquino said. "Will it be okay if you stay here? It might be better if I go in by myself."

"Of course, ma'am. I'll just see you to the gate."

I got out and helped Mrs. Aquino from the car. I rang the doorbell as she smoothed away the wrinkles on her dress. Then she rubbed her face, as if wishing she could also straighten the lines up there. She slung her purse securely over her shoulder and tried to correct her spine.

I was about to push the doorbell a second time when Mrs. Aquino stopped me. A maid in uniform had come out from the house, walking rather slowly.

"Magandang gabi," Mrs. Aquino said. "Is your mistress in?"

The maid's expression suddenly changed as she approached us.

She wiped her hands on her apron. "Good evening po, ma'am," she said. "Are they expecting us po?" She was using so many polite markers.

"Of course they are," I said. I got a cold stare from Mrs. Aquino.

"Yes, sir," the maid said. She was still wiping her hands on her apron even though they seemed to have dried. "I'm sorry, but the mistress has gone out."

"What time will she be back?" I asked.

"I don't really know," the maid said. "But as you can see, her car isn't here."

"It's okay, dear," Mrs. Aquino said. "Don't worry."

The maid seemed like she was about to turn around and head back. "Psst," I said, lowering my voice. "Can't we at least wait inside?"

The maid looked unsure.

"It's getting rather cold," I said. "I don't want anything bad to happen to her."

She looked at Mrs. Aquino and then nodded at me.

"Please do come in," the maid said. She opened the gate and escorted us up the driveway. "Just go straight, ma'am," she said, pointing to the main door.

Mrs. Aquino thanked her and then said to me, "Actually, Lito, maybe you should wait inside, too. This might take a while."

———

The maid served us tea in the living room, and though I'd personally have preferred to drink beer or soda at that hour, I thought the matching porcelain cup and saucer were more suited to the ambience, so I played along. There were paintings and statues of nude figures next to the saintlier, clothed ones. I believe we've all been conditioned to consider this the height of artistic taste. But why, I wonder, is Jesus never completely naked on the cross, as he probably really was when the Romans crucified him? Perhaps that would distract too many people from their prayers. Funny how confining our taboos can be.

Lots of gold everywhere here, as if Midas himself had stumbled in drunk one night and randomly touched things while trying to find his way through. Golden clocks and lampshades, gold-polished light switches, gold picture frames, a gold-and-crystal chandelier, gold-painted handrails, even the grand piano was draped loosely in yellow velvet with gold trimming. You name it—in that house, it was gold.

"Oh, the orchids!" Mrs. Aquino said, standing up. "My goodness." She slowly made her way to the far end of the living room, which was connected to a greenhouse much, much larger than hers in Manila. I wondered if she realized that she was still clutching her teacup in one hand. "May I?" she asked the maid, and the maid moved to open the glass door for her.

"Thank you," Mrs. Aquino said. "This truly means a lot to me."

The maid seemed a bit puzzled by Mrs. Aquino's sudden effusiveness but managed to use it to her advantage. "Yes, ma'am," she said. "Those flowers also mean a lot to my mistress. It's a pain to look after them, honestly. Please be so kind, ma'am, as to carefully appreciate them."

"I understand," Mrs. Aquino said.

I followed Mrs. Aquino's lead and stood up to do my own walking tour, though I confined myself to the living room. There were some photos on top of the piano. The maid must've thought I wanted to experiment with the keys, though, to tell you honestly, I cannot play an instrument or even sing, for the life of me. She came over right away and asked how she could "be of any help."

"I'm just admiring the family pictures," I said. "Do you have your own, by the way? Kids, I mean."

"Two daughters," she said. "And you?"

"A son," I said.

"Grandkids?" she asked.

"None," I said. "As far as I know."

She smiled. "I have several, including a pair of twins."

I hadn't expected to hear that, mainly because I'd placed her in her mid-twenties. Not that it would be impossible to have grandchildren at that age. But then I thought it more likely that she was probably older than I had earlier imagined. I must have checked her out from head to toe. I didn't mean to. But she clearly caught me in the act, because she said, "If you're wondering, I had mine when I was very young."

"I don't doubt that," I said. "I guess it's not a bad decision to have kids earlier in one's life." Immediately I felt like a fool for saying it, because the topic of pregnancy could be delicate, you know, especially coming from the opposite sex. The last thing I wanted was to insinuate or be presumptive.

But she didn't seem to mind. In fact, she said that she agreed, because she couldn't imagine having kids again. I said children are a nuisance until they grow up and leave the house, which is when you miss them the most and wish they could be small again.

"Ah, that's what grandkids are for," she said.

We left it at that. She went on to arrange the photo frames in a way that suggested a certain pattern had to be followed, perhaps to imply chronology or to expose the more flattering images of the family, a formula with which only she, and maybe her mistress, would be familiar.

There was a certain restraint to the maid's movements that somewhat reminded me of your mother. She had your mother's long, silky hair, which could be a liability in this line of work. Your mother always tied hers in a bun, though, whereas this maid let it all flow down. The maid had grace, yes, but she also had something else. Self-consciousness, I believe. She seemed to know, or affect to know, that she was being watched all the time. I don't think your mother ever felt that way, because she was always so consumed by what she was doing in the present.

I remember wondering how much of that self-consciousness came from the maid's personality, and how much had something to do with her employer. What must it be like to work for Imelda Marcos? Was she strict or easygoing? As someone who valued beauty above all else, did she expect her servants to uphold her standards of beauty as well? And what about her children? As I tried to look for clues in the family pictures, I played this scene in my mind:

Imelda and her children—her son and her daughters—go shopping for clothes. At every stop, she sits patiently on a chair and asks them to come out of the fitting room to model each ensemble for her inspection. "Yes!" she says, or "Try a size smaller," or "Tsk, tsk, tsk, how ugly." Perhaps those stores are closed to the public while they are inside. Or perhaps she isn't so patient. Perhaps she just says, "Take everything you want and let's try all of them at home." It could have been very fun—and terrifying—to have Imelda as your mother.

"How about her grandkids?" I asked the maid. "Do they visit here a lot?"

"Grandkid," the maid said. "Only one." She pointed to a picture of a boy whose smile revealed his two rabbit-sized front teeth.

"He's very cute," I said.

"He's passed," she said.

"Excuse me?"

"He's gone. It was a terrible accident. He drowned while swimming in the pool by himself. It was very difficult for all of us, but especially for my mistress."

"I feel so bad," I said. "I didn't know."

"It's okay," she said. "I wouldn't have expected you to know. It was a couple of years ago."

We were quiet for a while as I processed the information. I thought it a bit strange that I'd never heard about the accident.

"Where are Imelda's pictures, anyway?" I asked, suddenly realizing that I hadn't seen any. "Are you hiding them from us?"

She didn't laugh at my joke. "What do you mean—Imelda?"

"I meant to say Mrs. Marcos, of course. I'm sorry."

"What are you talking about?" she said.

"You know, your mistress." I picked up each of the pictures, one by one, completely messing up the order in which they had just been carefully placed. Not only could I not find Mrs. Marcos, but Mr. Marcos and the children were absent as well. None of the people in the pictures were familiar at all.

"Are we at the wrong house?" I said. I began to panic. I began to walk toward the greenhouse to fetch Mrs. Aquino, and then I saw her purse lying on the coffee table. I found the pink baronial envelope inside. "What's your address here, again?"

The maid told me. I showed her the envelope, how the address matched exactly, right below where it said "Imelda Marcos."

Now it was the maid's turn to look confused. She took the envelope and, before I could stop her, reached inside to pull out its contents. She shook her head.

"Here," she said. She pointed at the card, which looked a little frayed around the edges:

YOU ARE CORDIALLY INVITED TO A
WEDDING RECEPTION
MAY 1, 1954

"I don't understand," I said.

The maid motioned for me to inch forward to where we could catch a glimpse of Mrs. Aquino inside the greenhouse. Mrs. Aquino was seated on a bench, still holding her teacup. She seemed so small and frail, next to the orchid blooms and their hanging roots. In the artificial light, her dress looked a bit discolored, no longer the pristine white of that morning. She seemed to be smiling, too. And at certain points, I could see that her mouth was moving, as if she were talking to someone else.

But she was all alone.

"It happens, you know," the maid said. "Especially at her age."

"I don't believe it," I said. I shook my head and continued to stare at Mrs. Aquino.

"It happens to the best of us," the maid said.

Finally, I asked, "Do you have a phone I can borrow?"

————

Mrs. Aquino hadn't moved by the time I got back to the living room, as if she had turned into part of the greenhouse's décor, like the statue of an old, broken aristocrat, or perhaps a character from a Greek tragedy. I closed the glass door behind me and gently sat next to her on the bench. Arranged in rows in front of us were some plastic pots, which I imagined served as the plant nursery. I could see nothing beyond the windows but the dark void of the night.

"Ma'am," I said. "I'm ready whenever you are."

She turned to me and tipped her head, as if she had just then noticed my presence. Just as quickly, she gazed away.

"I always thought it would have taken place here," she said. "Though I always wonder how we would've all fit."

I didn't know what she was talking about, but I tried my best. "I guess things are never as we imagine them."

She said, "I didn't imagine it, Lito. I saw a photo of this room in *Mr. and Ms.* magazine some years ago. They were doing a feature on the Marcos house."

"The Marcos house, ma'am?"

"Well, that's what it used to be, before the Apostols bought it."

I showed Mrs. Aquino the card. She sighed.

"I'm sorry I had to drag you all the way here, Lito," she said. "Believe me, if I could've done this by myself, I would have. It's going to be hard for me to explain what I did without sounding so . . ." She paused to search for the right word.

"Crazy?" I said.

"I was thinking *selfish*," she said. "But, yes, that one works, too."

"Sorry, ma'am."

She asked to look at the card. I handed it to her in exchange for her teacup. The porcelain had turned cold.

"This was the first and the last letter I ever received from Mrs. Marcos," she said. "Actually, it's not even a letter, is it? At the time I didn't know them personally—neither Imelda nor Ferdinand. So why, I wondered, was I invited to their reception? I posed this same question to Ninoy, only to find out that he had also been invited."

Mrs. Aquino laughed nervously. "Did you know that my husband used to court Imelda? Of course, that was before he became my husband, before he'd even met me. It was very brief, from what I understand, and he always told me their breakup was mutual. No hurt feelings on either side. I don't know that I ever believed him. I certainly tried to. So when I got the invitation from Imelda that day, to be honest it threw me off balance. Ninoy and I had a fight. It wasn't our proudest moment, let's just put it that way."

I nodded.

"You have to remember that I was very young then. I was twenty-one when we married, just a few months after the Marcoses. The thought did occur to me that he might just be trying to upstage them, or perhaps to reassure me, to erase all my insecurities once and for all. You won't be surprised to know that we never ended up going to Imelda's wedding party. I'd never been to this house until now, but I've always wondered about it. I wondered how it could've fit so many people."

I said, "Perhaps, ma'am, they'd have used the outdoors. There's a nice big lawn."

"Perhaps you're right," Mrs. Aquino said. "But they did have another wedding reception afterward, at a proper hotel in Manila, with hundreds on the guest list. My husband and I weren't invited to that one."

Mrs. Aquino shifted in her seat and I could feel the slight tremor on the bench. She was still holding the card, but no longer looking at it. "Lito," she said. "This is what I've asked myself many, many times, for many, many years. What would've happened if we'd accepted the invitation and had come to see Imelda on her wedding day? What if she was actually trying to reach out to us, to reach out to me, but I was too self-absorbed to see that? Would we have become friends? Would I have become part of her inner circle? And would I later have been able to dissuade her from certain things? Would many lives have been spared? Would my husband have lived? Would he have seen our kids and grandkids grow up, and would I be spending my last days with him, instead of alone?"

"That's a lot of *if*s and *would have*s, ma'am," I said.

"Yes, I know," she said. "Still, I was the one who decided for us. I told my husband we shouldn't come to see Imelda. And I could never forgive myself for that."

It wasn't long before the glare of headlights outside flashed through the greenhouse windows and briefly blinded us. The maid announced that Mrs. Apostol had arrived, and we were shown back to the living room. Mrs. Apostol was a little shorter than Mrs. Aquino and seemed somewhat feistier. "Well, well, well," she said, "isn't this a surprise."

"I'm sorry, I should've called," Mrs. Aquino said. "But I wasn't sure if I could get out of the house until we were finally on the road. And we almost didn't make it."

Mrs. Apostol looked offended, shaking her head, before she burst out laughing. "I've always said you were welcome to visit me anytime here, maré. And I meant it."

"That's what I remembered, too," Mrs. Aquino said.

The two of them exchanged hugs. Mrs. Aquino then told her

about our trip, including the little incident with the overheating car. But she also omitted certain things, like the time we spent waiting at the church, or the help we got from the sugarcane farmer and his water buffalo. Perhaps she didn't want to worry her friend. Mrs. Aquino gave me all the credit, saying I was the hero of the day for managing to drive the old car up through the mountains.

"The hero deserves a reward, then," Mrs. Apostol said. "What about dinner?"

"Oh, we don't want to impose," Mrs. Aquino said. She'd only planned a day trip, she said, and opined that we'd already been quite a nuisance, disturbing our host at a most inconvenient hour.

"Nonsense," Mrs. Apostol said. She again insisted on dinner, and even doubled down, saying it would be unsafe to drive back to Manila right away, so we had better stay the night. Before Mrs. Aquino could respond, Mrs. Apostol continued, "Think about your driver. He must be absolutely exhausted. He needs his rest."

I was lying on my bed in the basement room, thinking about what a strange day it had been, when I heard several footsteps shuffling upstairs. I went to check on what was happening and immediately recognized familiar voices. Mrs. Aquino's two daughters had come to fetch her. They tried to keep it down, but I could still overhear their conversation. They were debating whether they should leave right then, in the middle of the night, or wait until the next day. I tiptoed a bit closer, so I could see them in the living room. Mrs. Aquino was seated on the couch, framed on either side by the backs of her two grown girls. I decided I didn't want to get involved, but just as I was about to return downstairs, the floor beneath me creaked. Mrs. Aquino noticed me. And I tell you, for the life of me, I shall never forget the look on her face when she saw me.

————————

So that was how your father's many years of service came to an abrupt end.

It was decided, after the weekend, that I should drive the Crown to Tarlac and leave it at the old house. At that time, it was still a matter of debate whether the car should be put in a museum or simply be disposed of at a junkyard. In any case, it was clear that they no longer wanted Mrs. Aquino to have her own vehicle.

It was further decided, after a few weeks, that, in light of my own advanced age, I would not be laid off but might continue to serve the family in some capacity. It was again a matter of debate whether I should serve as a groundskeeper at the old house, or remain a driver, but for one of the children instead. In any case, it was clear they no longer wanted me around Mrs. Aquino.

"Don't worry, Lito," Manang Dionisia said. I'd just parked the Crown in the garage, its final resting place. "I know Madam. As long as she breathes, she won't let you down. She'll see to it that you're taken care of. Believe me."

And maybe she was right. Maybe Mrs. Aquino really did have my back, and defended me whenever her children started to wonder whether my time had come. Maybe Mrs. Aquino said, "Lito is family. He'll always belong here with us."

But I didn't want to prolong their agony. I understood very

well where the children were coming from. And I didn't want them to resent their mother because of me. She had so many other things to worry about, not least of which was the cancer spreading in her colon. In fact, she wouldn't last the year.

I was able to see her one last time, inside her bedroom, after we'd gotten back to Manila from Baguio.

"Thirty-six years, hmm?" she said.

"Yes, ma'am," I said. "And I'd do it all over again if I had the chance." I paused. "Except, maybe, for this one particular journey."

She laughed. "But I thought we had fun."

"We did, ma'am. I didn't know you liked junk food so much."

"Shhh. It's our little secret."

She became serious then and held my hand. "Are you sure about this, Lito? It doesn't have to end this way, you know."

"I'm sure, ma'am."

"But can you really find another job? If not, how are you going to survive?"

"I'll manage, ma'am," I said. "I've always managed to survive."

11

I HAVEN'T BEEN able to write to you lately. They've operated on me again. A team of doctors and nurses, that is. They trucked me to the local hospital, or so I was told, since I was asleep for the most part. But now I'm back here in the care home.

"You were shaking all over," Milo said. "Do you remember?"

I said I did not. Seeing his face gave me a surprising amount of joy. I said, "I'm just glad to be home."

"So you think of this place as your home now, sir?"

"Is there any other? Besides, home is wherever my books are." I pointed to the box that had gathered some cobwebs in the corner of the room. "Do you mind?"

Milo slid the box over to me.

"There's a dictionary of etymology somewhere."

"This, sir?" He grabbed the thickest book he could find. I thanked him.

"*Sepsis, sepsis, sepsis.* The word has burrowed into my ears."

"It means an infection, sir."

I actually knew what the word meant, and that my kidneys

had it. I had heard it mentioned a few weeks before, and just this morning, one of the doctors—he didn't introduce himself, most of them don't—used the word again. He said, "You were knocked out for a day or two." Actually, he used the word *natulog*, which means "to have slept." I think he'd taken one look at me and thought I wouldn't have understood otherwise. So I replied, "Do you mean I was unconscious? Was I in a coma?" Only then did he explain my condition in the most accurate terms.

"*Sepsis* is Greek for 'rotten,'" I read aloud. "The same word was adopted in modern Latin."

"Interesting," Milo said.

"What's more interesting is the way the word sounds. It's a very fleeting one. *Sepsis*. It vanishes on the tongue the moment you say it. *Sepsis*. It makes you want to keep repeating it, as if, each time, you're ever closer to capturing it. Don't you get it?"

Milo was quiet. I realized I was being hard on him again. I don't know why, really. One moment I'm so happy to see him, and the next I'm being awfully pugnacious. I think it's my own way of coping.

"I guess you're wondering about the point of all this." I closed the dictionary. "There are thousands of words out there, and a lifetime surely isn't enough to look up each one of them. I admit they used to give me some comfort and pleasure. I liked the promise, or the idea of a promise, that I'd be able to use them one day, when I got the chance. Perhaps I wanted to prove something about myself. But now that I'm old and dying, I think I tend to agree with you, Milo. What's the point?"

"Well, sir, if you put it that way, then everything is an exercise in futility. Again, I'm just a nurse. But medically speaking, sir, everyone *is* aging and dying. Just at different rates. Besides, none of us know when our time is up."

Oh, Milo. I'm surely going to miss that boy.

I suppose we'll have to talk about the ending.

Not mine, I don't mean, at least not yet. I meant to the main story I was telling you, the "scoop." I wonder if your readers might think it too disappointing that the meeting between Mrs. Aquino and Mrs. Marcos never actually happened. They might feel as if they've just been taken along for a ride, no pun intended.

On the other hand, I'm also hoping that readers—like me—are a self-selecting bunch. Somehow, I think we tend to appreciate the truth more than a fiction, even if it isn't as exciting. After all, the written word is just a bunch of black ink on a blank page—nothing that could seriously compete, for example, with the colors on the big screen. Not that there's anything wrong with movies. I enjoy them, too. I guess reading requires us to use our brains a bit differently, a bit more patiently.

Now, I apologize if the scoop I promised earlier might not have been the boon that I initially made it out to be. Or at least it won't seem that way on the surface. Rarely does the title or subject of a story explain what the story is all about. Though many of your readers might first become interested because of the personalities involved, it's my hope that they will stumble upon something else, something that is far more essential.

In the end, whether or not Imelda Marcos showed up in Baguio doesn't really matter. Whether or not Mrs. Aquino went to Baguio also doesn't matter. Even Mrs. Marcos and Mrs. Aquino themselves don't matter. What truly matters in our story—well, I shall leave that up to you and your discerning readers to figure out.

With that being said, I must tell you something else.

I believe that Mrs. Aquino did, in fact, forgive Imelda Marcos that day. I'm not saying this lightly; I've given it a lot of thought. I've come to realize that there's a difference between forgiveness and redemption.

Forgiving someone can occur without the presence or even the permission of the guilty party. Sometimes the person being forgiven has already passed away, even if their sin continues to cause harm.

Redemption, on the other hand, lies outside the forgiver's realm. It lies entirely on the part of the person being forgiven. To be redeemed requires a penitent heart, an admission of guilt, and a sincere attempt to change. In our case, I wonder if it applies to Mrs. Marcos. To this day, I've yet to hear her or any member of her family admit to any wrongdoing. Instead, they insist that they're the victims of either propaganda or a colossal misunderstanding.

Of course, it would have been easier and more ideal to forgive someone who was ready for redemption. It's by far the more difficult and bitter task to forgive someone who's absent or unwilling to seek forgiveness. One has to find a way to make the act feel both meaningful and deserved. I'm convinced that this is what Mrs. Aquino did by traveling all the way to Baguio while she was very sick.

Sometimes, when I'm alone and have nothing better to do, I admit that I give in to Mrs. Aquino by sacrificing my memories of that day and offering her the chance at a sweeter epilogue. I imagine her inside the greenhouse, sipping her cup of tea, while the moon outside hangs on the horizon and the stars form their constellations.

"Can I join you?" Imelda says, entering the greenhouse. She's as stunning as ever, her nightgown curving upward on her shoulders in the shape of those distinct butterfly sleeves. But Mrs. Aquino isn't the slightest bit jealous, because she's a vision herself, in her brilliant white dress.

"I've been waiting," she says, motioning for Imelda to sit on the bench. "Your maid makes a good pot of tea."

"I'd have one myself but I'm trying to cut down. I don't know about you, but it's so much harder to fall asleep at our age."

"I have my spells," Mrs. Aquino says.

"Well, what do we have here?" Imelda plucks the bud of a yellow orchid, the stem of which is stooping from its own weight.

"No touching, ma'am," Mrs. Aquino says.

Imelda laughs. "I do whatever I want," she says. "I deserve it. All year long I take care of them. Then they bloom, and in a week they're gone."

Mrs. Aquino thinks about her own flowers at home.

"I'm like that little prince," Imelda says, "who falls in love with a rose. There are hundreds and hundreds of roses out there, but there's only one that's special. Because it's mine.

"I'm sorry about your rose," she says.

Imelda hands Mrs. Aquino the orchid. It has a clean fragrance, almost like fresh fabric on a clothesline.

"Can you still find it in your heart to forgive this old woman?"

And Mrs. Aquino would say, "I can. I've already done so. Long before you asked."

12

YOU KNOW, AFTER I retired from service, the Aquinos gave me a considerable sum, enough to sustain me for a year or two before I had to look for work again. You might wonder what I did with my time. Well, I created a version of Walden Pond in my own apartment. I stocked up on books and food and various supplies, so I'd have little need to go outside. I planted a few potted vegetables that required very little care, other than when I wanted to harvest them. I became, in short, a loafer. I'd like to think I was the kind of productive loafer that exists in all of us—a man in his natural state, if the world were still as unbroken as Eden.

I had held on to many of my schoolbooks, and I began to read them again. It's amazing how different they are when seen through an adult's eyes, perhaps especially when that adult is on the older side. I laughed at the lessons that I'd never had use for in my life, because they tended to be the ones that the teacher once emphasized the most. Things like the Pythagorean theorem; the year in which the bubonic plague broke out; the names of major and minor characters in *Noli me tángere*. It's not at all that I object to studying mathematics or history or literature. It's that we were led to believe that the information itself is crucial, when it's how to use the information that's the key. All education or learning should help us get closer to the truth of our reality. It should equip us with a way to test whether what we're thinking is closer to, or farther from, the truth. If it doesn't do that, then education is useless. This becomes obvious, I think, with technology. The challenge is no longer how to access information, but what to do when we're swimming in it. How can we discern truth from fiction, and how can we benefit from either?

Speaking of the internet, I did try to take some college courses online. They were free. And they gave me an experience I've always been curious about but could not otherwise have afforded. I took sociology, for instance, with a professor in Copenhagen, as one of the thousands of students who "sat" in his virtual class. We studied classical thinkers, the likes of Mandeville and Weber, by way of Smith and Marx. I'd had occasion to grapple with that last one, of course, a few times in my life.

One day I even wrote the professor an email, more out of a desire to clarify my own thoughts than because I expected a reply. But reply he did, to my surprise. That led to another email from me and then from him, until we struck up a real conversation and, I daresay, a friendship. Anyway, I won't bore you with the details, except that it led me to conclude that Marx and Marcos are actually quite similar, not just in ideology and the means to their ideology, but also in their willful blindness. This blindness was what caused each man to believe in the goodness of his respective solution—the rule of the proletariat, for one, and the New Society, for the other. It was also why neither thought to erect any mechanism whatsoever, no circuit breakers, so to speak, to keep his solution in check. The result: an unattainable utopia.

"Do you think it's a coincidence that both systems led to authoritarian leaders?" the professor wrote me. "And just to play devil's advocate," he added, "why aren't dictators a good thing? Don't they usually achieve results more quickly?"

I had to admit I hadn't thought deeply about the merits of dictatorships. I'd always assumed they were a bad thing. After a few days of pacing in my room, I came up with a tentative answer.

"In my experience," I wrote back, "it's because they require us to put our complete trust in them, as if they were gods who cannot be questioned. But dictators are only human. And the minute we give ourselves up to them completely is the minute they become our abusers. It would be the exception rather than the norm to wind up with a 'noble dictator,' if there really is such a thing—one with true wisdom, a good heart, and the right amount of willpower. In my humble opinion, it's just not worth the risk of the bad apples."

I know I'm being tedious again by trying to be smart about things you're probably already well aware of. What I meant to emphasize earlier was that I was quite happy in my own solitude. I would, for example, spend many days lost in the computer, often on Wikipedia, clicking incessantly from one article to another, until the sun went down and my eyes started to hurt.

I remember Manang Dionisia once called me to see how I was doing. She said, "Why don't you leave your house for a while and get some fresh air? Maybe we can go on a short holiday together."

I said, "Why would I ever do that? If I go outside, I have to face three enemies, while inside I only have one."

"Whatever are you talking about now, Lito?"

"Beyond these walls I have to worry about finding my breakfast, lunch, and dinner. Here, I worry only about how to prepare them."

She laughed at that one. And I'd even forgotten to factor in snacks.

In my aimless quest for learning, eventually I stumbled upon the possibilities of the future, or what our society today thinks of as the future. Cryptocurrency, for example. Though I still don't understand the underlying technology, I am particularly susceptible to its promise as a way to inhibit corrupt banks and governments. In addition, I dream of a world where a person has the freedom to move as he pleases, and to go to any country where he'd like to become a citizen. That might starve all the despots and inept rulers of the one true resource, the one they constantly underestimate to their detriment—their own people.

But perhaps what amuses me the most is the idea of cars driving themselves. I can see how that might lead to safer roads, because robots never get distracted or need to sleep. But I also wonder, Would they be as companionable to their passengers? Would they know when to be polite and reserved and when to be funny? Could they reminisce and opine on life and our mortality? Well, I guess I'm still old-fashioned that way. There are certain things that I'd rather not tamper with. I don't have to worry, of course, because I won't be around long enough to find out, or to complain. You'll have to stop by my grave and let me know.

Last week I had the rare chance to talk to your mother again over the phone, and when I asked where you were, she said you'd gone on an errand, to a place called Half Moon Bay, and that it would probably take you a few more days. She didn't tell me what the errand was, of course, but I wouldn't forget such a peculiar name for a place.

You know, I've lost count of how many letters I've written to you. When I first started, I remember your mother mentioning that her purple peonies had just bloomed. She was never one to like flowers or all the other things that girls are supposed to like. She often used to say that people's expectations of others are usually unfair. In this, your mother and I are very similar. We like to defy people and their expectations.

"How are you anyway?" she asked. "I mean, how are you, truly?"

I could hear an engine revving and then your mother apologizing, saying that she was on the cordless. She was outside on the front porch, and your neighbor had just pulled out of the garage.

"No need to apologize," I said. "Is it a nice day there?"

"Depends on your definition," she said. "It's hot. It's summer again."

"I used to hate heat," I said.

"And now?"

"I hate it even more."

She laughed. "Me, too."

I asked your mother what she had been up to those days. And so she told me about the gutter that was clogged and needed fixing. She talked about going to the roof to clear the needles that had fallen off your pine tree. She talked about the squirrels that kept eating the seeds she intended for the birds. I couldn't help but smile at the idea of her chasing down some furry rodent.

It's a delicate kind of peace, what your mother and I have achieved over the years. So I listened to her every word and I tried to imagine her life there with you. After she finished talking about her peonies, all wilted now in the heat, I asked if she would be okay with me divulging another secret. Because there was something else I'd forgotten that I wanted to tell you. One final story that concerns you.

———

Your mother is the light of my life. Trite, I know, but it's true. I've never said this to her outright, and I don't think I'll start the habit now. It's just going to have to be between you and me. That's how some things are meant to be.

The first time I met your mother, she was stooped at the staircase of the old house, a rag in her hand. My first words to her were "You have wood polish on your neck." She smiled. People have always talked about that smile, how soft her cheeks were and how beautiful her face. To be honest, those things didn't occur to me until much later. No, what struck me then was something shallower: she seemed to take an immediate liking to me, even when we barely knew each other. That goes a long way, you know, for someone as young and naïve as I was back then.

From the start, our relationship was cloaked in secrecy. The matriarch of the house, Doña Aurora, watched our every move. There was nothing special about this, because she watched everyone with the same interest. She was like a cop on the lookout for any hint of wrongdoing. That made things a bit difficult for me and your mother. We were very careful. We'd hide under the stairwell just to talk, or in the kitchen, where I'd find her washing dishes after each meal. It was there, after I'd given her some chocolates from the city, that I received my first kiss: a rather messy, soapy surprise.

Things became a lot easier when your mother moved to Manila with me. Mrs. Aquino was more liberal with days off. She was also very busy, not just with the children, but also with the lawyers who were trying to get her husband out of jail. Still, we played it safe, your mother and I. We didn't know what would happen if Mrs. Aquino found out about us. Most employers aren't keen on their servants getting into relationships. They might think that we'd become less productive. Or that we'd take our leaves of absence at the same time. Worse, they might think that we'd conspire to steal or to overpower them if we were unhappy. We might lose our jobs.

"I wish we could just go away somewhere," she said, "and be ourselves."

"What do you think we're doing now?" I said. We were walking beside the fountain in a park, her hand in mine. It had rained, and the night was a little cool.

"I meant somewhere far away."

I was quiet.

"Hey," she said. "I don't mean to remind you of that."

"I know," I said. She was, of course, referring to my father, who'd just stopped talking to me then. At the time he was always on my mind, him and the mountains. I said, "I just love to be dramatic, don't I?"

She laughed. Then she said, "If you could go anywhere in the world, where would you choose?"

"What about Havana?"

"Isn't that in South America?" she said. "Why? What's there?"

"Plenty," I said. "The music is great, for one."

"How do you know all that?"

"I've been there," I said. "And, I'm sorry to say, Cuba is actually in North America."

"I'm impressed," she said.

Later, I hailed a cab and asked the driver to take us to the Silahis Hotel. Your mother was a bit perplexed, until we reached the top of the hotel, and there, in garish red letters, was CAFÉ HAVANA.

"Ah!" your mother said. "You're corny!"

I admit it was a terrible joke. But while we were at the club, we pretended to be socialites. We drank all our drinks with those little foldable umbrellas and tipped our pinkie fingers.

"Isn't this what you always wanted?" I asked. "We're finally being our true selves."

"Here's to us being dons and doñas! Though I think you're playing the part of doña much better. Look at that finger."

I clinked her glass. "I'll drink to that."

"Lito," she said, "would you care to dance with me?"

I said I didn't know how to, and I was afraid I'd embarrass her. "Just come," she said. "Will you?"

She pulled me to the dance floor before I had a chance to say no. There we stood, right next to the speakers where the disco music played the loudest, one song after another, on and on, as if they'd been spliced together so those of us dancing wouldn't have reason to stop. And there was not much talking, either, because we couldn't possibly hear much else. We just held on, closer and closer to each other, until all I could feel were her arms around me, her lips squarely on my mouth and sometimes on my neck. It didn't matter where she placed them, because it was so dark and nobody knew who we were or what we were doing. That night was a good night for both of us.

———

One day, as I drove Mrs. Aquino and her kids to see their grandmother in Tarlac, your mother asked me to stop the van. I hadn't completely pulled over yet when she opened the window and let out a volley of fluids. When we got to the old house, Manang Dionisia took your mother to her room so she could rest.

"Is she ill?" I asked. "It must be something we ate along the way. Her stomach gets upset easily."

I waited until Manang Dionisia came out and closed the door. In a low voice, she said, "Lito, what have you done?"

I said I didn't know what she was talking about.

She stared hard at me, but when she saw that I really had no clue, she sighed. "You better tell Madam," she said. "Sooner or later, it'll be obvious, and everyone will know."

"What? Is she . . . ?"

Manang Dionisia shook her head. "Do you even realize what you've gotten yourselves into?"

I was quiet.

"Never mind," she said. "Just do as I tell you."

I said I would. But I pleaded for more time to think about the best way forward.

She nodded. And then she went back inside the room.

As it was, I never did get to tell Mrs. Aquino. In fact, I never told anyone. How Manang Dionisia found out about that night is beyond me. Perhaps she had seen us together inside that house, and she'd sensed certain things the way only Manang Dionisia could. Or perhaps your mother had confessed to her. If so, however, that happened only once.

Because, as the weeks passed into months, I did the most natural and stupid thing a man could do. I asked if she wanted to make it go away, so we could get back to where we'd left off. I said all the usual stuff about being young and ambitious and not throwing away the future, hers or mine.

"But what about preserving this future?" she asked, touching her belly.

"It's not too late," I said. "We can try again when we're both ready."

"I see," she said.

"You understand, there's just too much going on right now. It's far too complicated."

"I do," she said. "It's a pity."

"I hope you know I care about you."

She looked me in the eye. And then she said, "You're a coward, Lito."

I waited for her to continue. But instead, she turned around and gathered up her cleaning supplies. She said, "I have a lot of work to do."

———————

Mrs. Aquino eventually noticed your mother's bump. I was about to leave town for the weekend when I walked by the two women outside the greenhouse and heard her tell your mother that she had gained a lot of weight. I quickly hid behind the corner of the garage. She asked if everything was all right, and when your mother didn't say anything, she asked her to go inside the house so they could talk. I decided to wait.

I was, of course, very scared. Scared about losing our jobs, scared that Mrs. Aquino would find out the truth, and scared of the immense shame that would fall upon me on her discovery. Having a child out of wedlock was a bigger taboo back then, and though I did not care for the Church, I cringed at the thought of Mrs. Aquino's opinion of me. I was completely self-absorbed. I did not even think of the physical changes that your mother was going through. I knew of the emotional ones, and I sympathized with her on that front, believe me. But the pain and discomfort from the pregnancy, and later on from the incomparable agony of labor, those things somehow eluded me. I wasn't only a coward, it turned out, but also callous and a fool.

An hour or so later, your mother came out of the house, and I could see that she had been crying. I knew I had no right to ask about their conversation. I wondered if she had lost her job, and if she had involved me in the process. She didn't seem to notice me, and I decided to pack up my bags.

I left that afternoon to catch the last bus to Moncada. While

I was at my father's, all I could think about was how I had managed to fail at everything. The people I was once closest to, both relatives and friends, no longer wanted to talk to me. At the time I didn't think that it was entirely my fault. I thought I was a victim of circumstance, and I felt trapped and cursed by my fate. But as Monday rolled around and I returned to work, I saw that your mother was still there. She was mopping the kitchen floor and singing. Things seemed to be back to normal. And I was relieved.

One morning, Mrs. Aquino said she had something important to tell me. I had just picked her up from Fort Bonifacio, where her husband was imprisoned. He had then just announced a hunger strike to protest the final result of his military trial, which had found him guilty of subversion, among other things, and had him sentenced to death by a firing squad. He had already been in solitary confinement for five years. Naturally, I thought she would give me some details about his condition. Instead, she told me about *her* condition, your mother's.

"I'm hoping that we can show her our support," Mrs. Aquino said. "She really needs it now. I know for a fact that people are going to talk and call her all sorts of names."

I said that I understood.

"Good," she said. "You know, if there's someone who deserves any ill treatment, it's that reckless man who did this to her and then disappeared. If I had my way, I'd track him down. But . . ." Mrs. Aquino sighed. "She doesn't want me to. It was an accident, she said. She blames herself for it, poor girl. But she needs to focus on the child now. I promised I'd help however I can. I trust you will, too, Lito."

"Of course, ma'am."

Not long after that, I drove your mother and Mrs. Aquino to the clinic. They looked very excited when they got back to the car. Mrs. Aquino was saying that she could go through her closet and find some old baby clothes. She said she didn't think there'd be another one coming for her.

"Did you hear the good news, Lito?" Mrs. Aquino said. "The doctor showed us the pictures. She's going to have a healthy boy."

"Oh wow," I said. "That's wonderful. Congratulations."

"Thank you," your mother said. After a pause, she added, "Actually, I think I've settled on a name, too."

"Did you, now?" Mrs. Aquino said.

I adjusted the rearview mirror. "May I ask what it is?"

Then she uttered it, the name that belonged to my father. And as Mrs. Aquino admired its nice, classic ring, I could see that your mother was smiling.

I always thought that she did it to spite me, to taunt me. Because I hadn't told anyone else about my father. So in a way she was betraying my trust, mocking all the confessions I had made to her. I know I deserved it. I am not seeking sympathy here. In fact, I mention it only because now I believe that your mother had another motive in choosing that name. Despite her stiff upper lip, I think she must've been crying out for help.

She was only twenty-two when she gave birth to you, the adorable baby boy that everyone fell in love with at first sight.

You fit in with the Aquino children so effortlessly. They took turns rocking you back and forth in the crib, as if you were one of them. You and your mother were showered with compassion and gentleness and an abundance of affection.

After everyone had had their chance to meet you and the house became quiet again, she swaddled you in the blanket and offered you up to me. I hesitated, because I'd never held a baby before in my life and I was afraid I might drop you. But when your mother handed you to me, and you instantly clung to my shoulders with those tiny hands of yours, I thought: all the trouble in the world for this one little boy, and yet I had been wrong—very wrong.

What manner of man would I be if, after holding my own flesh and blood, I remained unaffected? I did cry when you were in my arms. Even your mother seemed startled. She took you back and told me that I needed to control myself.

———

But we grew to like each other, you and I.

"Uncle," you'd say, because that was what your mother taught you to call me, once you were big enough to talk. "When are we going to the mall again?"

"Right now," I'd say.

"Right now?"

"This very second." I'd look at my watch.

"But I haven't even eaten breakfast."

"That's too bad."

"Can you wait?"

"Sure. Ten, nine, eight . . ."

"Uncle, stop it!" And then you'd run to the door to block off my passage. You were just a runt trying to beat back a fat grown man like me, and yet somehow, I wasn't able to pass.

"All right," I'd say. "You win. I give up. I'll wait for you."

———

There were times along the way when I was prepared to tell everyone about you. The thing with secrets, you see, is that the effort required to hide them sometimes becomes as unbearable as the terrible things we imagine might happen with their revelation. But it was your mother who stopped me.

She said, "Don't you think it's a little late for that? How are you supposed to make things better now?"

"Well," I said, "the boy could use a father, for a start."

"Oh, how very gracious of you to offer."

But she did change her tone.

She said, "Let's just wait a bit and see what happens with this arrangement."

Indeed, for a while it seemed that you might be better off without me. You and your mother were getting by just fine. And the people around us—at least the people who really mattered—seemed to have forgotten the whole business with the unexpected pregnancy. It was almost as if your mother had given divine birth. My confession, even if it were the truth, would only serve to disturb a settled issue.

But then your mother came up with a brilliant solution. This was around the time when Mr. Aquino suffered a heart attack while in prison. We were all afraid that he wouldn't make it. Mrs. Aquino, especially, took to praying at all hours of the day, and would invite anyone with a pulse to join her. The entire household seemed to have come to a halt. It felt as if we were rehearsing our parts before a wake.

I was in the garage, trying to fix the old van, which itself seemed to be nearing its end, when your mother appeared and said she wanted to talk to me. We sat inside the van and closed the doors.

"I've been thinking," she said. "What if we move on from our past and have a fresh start?"

I said, "That sounds good. But is it possible?"

"What if you don't need to admit to anything, except perhaps that you want to become the father from now on and be head of the family?"

I said I did not understand.

"Marry me, Lito," she said. "And then you can adopt us. We can finally have our family."

If there ever were a moment in my life when I was offered a chance at a turning point, that clearly would have been it. If I were a character in a story, all the successes and failures leading up to that point would've been part of my training to equip me to make this one crucial decision. And that decision, in turn, would determine whether my story would be a heroic epic, or a tragedy.

I don't know what to tell you. Except that in reality, while we're making these decisions, we never know if we're still in the lead-up or already at the point of no return. I always thought I had more time. That's one of the bigger flaws of my character.

Another is that I constantly abuse the grace of the people around me until it's too late.

I don't always mean to. Most of the time, I think, I'm rather oblivious. I lack the self-awareness that turns an ordinary person into a saint, or, in my case, even just a decent man. Isn't it ironic that, in order to be selfless, one first has to be self-aware? I don't mean the kind of self-consciousness that a teenager might have. I mean a deep understanding of oneself, one's privileges, one's shortcomings. I don't seem ever to have found that, I'm afraid. Unless, maybe, in retrospect, years and years later.

And so I turned down your mother's offer. Arrogant of me, I know. I can't really begin to explain why I did it. But I do want to try, if you allow me. I *must* try. Because otherwise you might think—if you haven't already—that it had something to do with you. Or your mother. That the two of you were somehow not good enough for me. When, in fact, any defect lies solely with me.

I am my father's son. And all my life I've tried not to become who he was: someone so consumed by his wife, or the idea of her, at the expense of everything else. I have wished many times that he'd never met her, so that I'd never have been born. If I'd never been born, then I'd never have been left to myself, never have had to fend off the cruel boys at the boarding school, never have been driven off to live up in those mountains, where I became so broken. But not in a million years did I imagine that I'd turn out to be worse than my father. Because not only did I abandon you and your mother, but I never even acknowledged either one of you as mine.

Forgive me. For failing to recognize this when I had the chance to make a difference. For not having been there for you and your mother and for causing so much harm. I sent both of you into exile, I see that now. Because the life you'd have lived here would certainly have been far more difficult and painful with me in the picture. Forgive me for staying quiet for so long. And for suddenly reaching out to you in this way, when I am old and decrepit, and you are too far away to have the chance to do anything. I really am asking too much, aren't I? These past few weeks, in exchange for years and years of my silence and neglect.

How I wish to see you and your mother one last time. This hope, you know, was what sustained me after my heart momentarily stopped and I fell down a flight of stairs. I say this not so you'll feel something for me. Considering how badly I've messed up, I've lived a good life, all in all. Thank you, rather, for staying with me long enough and for tolerating my stories, incoherent and rambling though they may be. I hope you can use some of them. And if not, then I hope something still comes of this. Finally knowing the plain truth, perhaps. Or as admonition to steer clear of your father's example—though I've set the bar quite low on that one.

I love you, son. And I love your mother as I've never loved anyone else. It's difficult for me to say this, but I think your mother also felt the same way, at least for a time. She has a partner but she never married, as you know, even if it would've been more convenient, for her and for you. It took me a while to realize this myself. And then a few more decades passed before I could finally admit that she still loved me. Well, I am a slow learner. Who knows what little else I'd discover if I had another few decades to spare? Take good care of her, now. Take good care of yourself.

This morning, Manang Dionisia visited me in my crypt of a bed. No pork sandwiches this time. Food is strictly forbidden. It's all liquids from here on out, until the surgery, which I think will be my last.

I told her that I'm saying goodbye to you.

She said, "I'm afraid I've come to do the same thing, just in case."

"So this is a send-off party."

She smiled. "I'd rather think of it as a welcome-home party. If things do take a turn for the worse."

"You know I don't actually believe in any of that stuff."

"Stubborn to the end, I see. I guess you won't let me pray for you, either."

"I'd rather you didn't," I said. "But thank you."

She nodded.

"You know this isn't my first time. I've come close to it at least once before." I stretched the collar of my gown and showed her the welt on my neck. "Have I ever told you? I was waiting inside the truck when it happened. I'd just delivered the early morning crates of bread. That was my job for a few years after retiring, remember? Delivering pandesal for this bakery chain all over Manila."

"I remember," she said.

"Anyway, as I was parked at the docking bay outside the mall, I heard gunshots. And then the craziest thing happened. Some masked men came running toward me. I heard people shouting, this time from the back of the truck. I hid in the driver's seat but

I could make out policemen in the side mirror, a good dozen of them maybe. I was shaking in my shoes. They exchanged more fire and then I passed out. When I woke up I was behind bars with a bandage hastily wrapped around my neck."

"It was a bank robbery, wasn't it?" Manang Dionisia said. "And they took you for an accomplice."

"Yes," I said. "A bunch of idiots."

"I was ill at that time, Lito. Otherwise, I'd have come to the station and fetched you myself."

I waved her off. "I only remembered bits and pieces from when I was unconscious. But the feeling was distinctly that of drowning. It was very dark and I couldn't breathe. I kept wanting to surface. I kept thinking, Not yet, not yet."

"Some people might say you were given a second chance."

"That's a nice use of the passive," I said. "Can you clarify by whom?"

"By whomever you want!" She seemed exasperated.

"I'm sorry, Manang," I said. "I agree with you. I did have a second chance. I was very fortunate."

Her eyes danced around the room but managed to avoid mine.

Just like that, we were back on our familiar, awkward ground.

"I have one last question," I said. "If I may."

"Go on."

"I've always wondered why you never told anyone about me. You know, about my sin. Why didn't you ever put me in my place?"

"Must we really talk about that now?"

I said, "Might as well."

She drew a long breath. Then she said, "My heart breaks

every time I think of it. You were very, very young then, Lito. And, to be honest, I didn't know what was worse: forcing a reluctant boy to swallow his bitter pill, or leaving your child to grow up on his own. Either way, it seemed to me, would bring pain."

I nodded.

"You and your aunt could've fooled other people," she said, "but I knew the truth. I knew that license of yours was forged to begin with. You couldn't have been eighteen at the time you applied for the job. I don't think so."

"I was sixteen," I said.

"Don't get me wrong. There are men around that age, and plenty of women, who could take on such a big responsibility. But you weren't one of them, Lito. I'm afraid you wouldn't have been a good parent."

"No, I probably wouldn't."

"Still," she said. "Perhaps you could've tried. Perhaps I should've made you. But I also promised your aunt I'd let no harm fall on you. Perhaps I did wrong."

We were quiet for a while.

"Comforter," I began, "where, where is your comforting? Mary, mother of us, where is your relief?"

"Are you reciting a prayer," she asked, "or a tongue-twister?"

"A poem," I said. "At least trying to. But I've forgotten the rest of it." She laughed. "I should know better by now than to break out in poetry, especially when my mind's no longer what it used to be."

"None of ours are," she said.

I was still trying to remember those lines.

"So," she said. "In your own understanding, what do you think comes next?"

"Nothing," I said. "I cease to be."

"Just like that?" she asked. "Isn't that quite sad?"

"Maybe," I said. "But I think it's the truth. And besides, how you feel won't matter after you're dead."

"I don't know about that," she said. "I think I'd like to be able to see certain people who have once passed on."

"Like who? Mrs. Aquino?"

"I wasn't thinking of her. But, yes, why not—Madam, too."

"I doubt I'll have that chance," I said. "And you know what? I'm fine with it. I'm fine with nothingness."

"You're a brave man after all," Manang Dionisia said.

"No lingering! Let me be fell: force I must be brief!" I took Manang Dionisia's hand and shook it in triumph. "I remembered it, Manang! I remembered my poem!"

"Or maybe just a very foolish one," she said.

"Either way," I said, smiling, "we'll find out soon enough."

ACKNOWLEDGMENTS

This book evolved from a screenplay to its current form as a novel. To each and every person who helped me get here, I am deeply indebted:

V. V. Ganeshananthan and Eileen Pollack, for their mentorship and constant support, and for reading the novella version when it was barely readable.

Margot Livesey and Lan Samantha Chang, for their invaluable guidance at the Iowa Writers' Workshop; Paul Harding, for his generosity and inspiration; Sasha Khmelnik and Drew Calvert, my Iowa buddies.

Thank you to my agents, Ellen Levine and Alexa Stark, and my editors at Farrar, Straus and Giroux, Julia Ringo and Milo Walls, for believing in me and making this book possible.

Laurianne Uy, who read early drafts of this novel while on a bumpy train ride in Italy.

For community and friendship, John Bengan and the DWG.

Work on this book was supported by the generous David T. K. Wong, who gave me the best year of my writing life, in the UK, where most of this novel was written.

Finally, to my family; I am grateful for their patience and love.